LIGHT THE CANDLES

Who is the attractive stranger who knocks on the Cornells' door one snowy Christmas Eve? Lucy discovers the answers to a tragic family secret — and finds lifelong romance . . . Charlotte and Bill are happily married — until they have children, forcing Charlotte to choose between being a loving wife or a caring mother . . . Nicholas Carden is impossibly handsome — and a woman-hater. But Victoria is determined to marry him, by hook or by crook! Twelve tales of the heart by veteran author Denise Robins.

DENISE ROBINS

◆

LIGHT THE CANDLES
and Other Stories

Complete and Unabridged

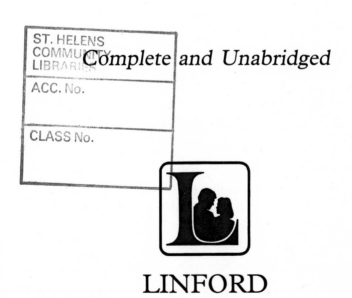

LINFORD
Leicester

First published in Great Britain in 1959

First Linford Edition
published 2015

A catalogue record for this book is available
from the British Library.

ISBN 978–1–4448–2408–7

Published by
F. A. Thorpe (Publishing)
Anstey, Leicestershire

Set by Words & Graphics Ltd.
Anstey, Leicestershire
Printed and bound in Great Britain by
T. J. International Ltd., Padstow, Cornwall

This book is printed on acid-free paper

Contents

Light the Candles

1

The Christmas-tree stood in a corner of the room.

It was dark in the big drawing-room on this grey, dreary day of December the twenty-fourth. The tree stood in shadow. Faintly the tinsel glittered and the coloured glass balls could only pick up fragments of light. The wax candles looked like little twisted sugar-sticks in their toy tin holders.

Lucy, gazing from the doorway, thought of all the hours she had spent in decorating the tree. She sighed; sighed again at the sight of the holly behind the gilt-framed pictures on the walls, at the crossed loops of gay-coloured paper nailed from end to end of the room, at the big bunch of mistletoe tied with scarlet ribbon hanging from the crystal chandelier.

It was all so festive, and yet so cold

and dark — so utterly lacking in any gaiety. Like the big Victorian house itself, which was always silent and full of ghosts. True, it was all quite comfortable, even luxurious in the manner of the last generation. Mrs Cornell had spared no money when she had come here as a young bride. And nothing had been changed. The walls were still hung with the dark crimson-striped paper. Like the thick carpet with its floral design, the satin-wood chairs and tables, the heavy brocade curtains, the Venetian blinds.

Lucy was used to it all. She had lived here with her aunt for the last ten years, since the death of her own parents had left her an orphan. In a way she liked the old house, mainly because it meant so much to Aunt Madge. Poor Aunt Madge, who had nothing but her memories — and Lucy — to comfort her now that she was failing fast in health, both mentally and physically.

Aunt Madge had money. There were servants — old retainers — to do all the work at Blakeley Grange.

But sometimes Lucy wished that she had more to do. She was so unutterably bored. Here she was, aged twenty-one, the bosom companion of an old lady who had grown 'queer' since The Tragedy of more than twenty years ago. (The Tragedy that was only spoken of every Christmas Eve.) There were no young friends for Lucy, no dances, no parties. Nothing would happen here today or tomorrow to warrant all these Christmas decorations. The tree which stood there in its fairy-like splendour must remain in darkness. The candles would never be lit. That was all part of The Tragedy.

Tomorrow morning there would be a present for Lucy — a handsome present from Aunt Madge. Then church. A Christmas dinner for the two of them. (That was always a mockery!) And after that a walk. Tea and the effort to help Aunt Madge forget the past. Good night, and then the prospect of another difficult year. Lucy wondered how many more of them she could bear before she ran away!

She walked to the windows and peered out. It was past five o'clock and darkness had fallen. All day snow had threatened. Now it was falling, whirling in grey feathery flakes against the panes. In the morning the cedar which stood on the wide lawns outside Blakeley Grange would be a lovely sight.

The silence was broken suddenly by the crunch of footsteps on the gravel drive. Who could that be at this hour? There were few callers at the Grange, except Aunt Madge's doctor and one or two local friends who had known the Cornells for years.

Lucy turned back to the drawing-room and switched on the light. At once the vast crystal chandelier flung out a myriad shooting-stars, flooding the whole room with magnificence.

A moment later, old Florence, the parlourmaid who had been with Mrs Cornell ever since The Tragedy, came in.

'Please, miss, could you come and talk to a gentleman who is in need of help and wants to use the telephone?'

'But, Florence,' said Lucy, 'you know we are not on the telephone.'

'I know, miss. But the gentleman seemed so surprised and upset. Will you speak to him?'

With sudden recklessness, Lucy said: 'Ask him in, Florence.'

A tall young man was ushered into the drawing-room. He stood, hat in hand, looking at Lucy. She looked back at him. She had to admit that he was exceedingly good-looking. So tall, and with such square shoulders, black hair and bright hazel eyes.

He smiled at her. 'I'm afraid I'm intruding,' he said. 'But my car has let me down, and I seem to have struck the loneliest part of the world for my breakdown. I could hardly believe it when the maid said that you were not on the 'phone.'

'My aunt is old-fashioned and doesn't like the disturbance of the bell

7

ringing,' explained Lucy.

'This is your aunt's house?'

'Yes. Mrs Cornell. I am Lucy Cornell, her niece.'

'My name is John Mostyn,' he said.

He was a friendly young man with a wide, friendly smile, and Lucy could not resist it. The shadows seemed to have lifted in this room. Not only because of the light from the chandelier. She felt suddenly happy. A dimple appeared at the corner of her mouth. John Mostyn, with his six-foot-two of good looks, was standing right under the mistletoe opposite her. She wondered if he noticed the fact.

Blushing, she backed away a bit and said: 'What bad luck for you to have broken down.'

But he felt that it was good luck, because he had never seen a prettier girl than this one. And she was naturally pretty, not in an artificial way. No heavy make-up, only a touch of lipstick. He was ready to swear that there was no mascara on the long, dark lashes of Miss

Lucy Cornell. She had two brown plaits of hair pinned round her small head, and large dark, fawn-like eyes. She was small and slender in her cherry-coloured woolly dress. He noticed that entrancing dimple when she smiled.

'I'm darned if I know what to do,' he said. 'How far are you from the nearest garage? This is my first visit to England and to Devonshire. I was driving around intending to spend my Christmas wherever I landed. Where have I landed, by the way?'

'On the outskirts of Exmoor,' she said. 'And the nearest garage is ten miles away.'

'Lord!' he groaned. 'Then it's a ten-mile tramp for me in the snow, and no food yet awhile.'

'Oh dear,' said Lucy with distress. 'You can't walk through the snow, when you don't know your way or anything. It's frightfully lonely around here. I must tell my aunt. She'd never let you do that.'

'Please — I wouldn't dream — ' he began.

Then a voice interrupted them. A rather high-pitched, tremulous voice.

'But it *may* be André, Florence. You wouldn't remember him. I ought to know. I saw him walking up the drive from my window. I *know* it's André. Let me see him. Help me down. Call Miss Lucy quickly.'

John Mostyn looked at Lucy. She answered his unspoken question, her cheeks pink and hot.

'That's my aunt. I must explain to you quickly. She — she isn't quite normal. You heard what she said. She thinks you may be André. That's her son. My cousin. There was an awful Tragedy . . . '

'I'm so sorry. But please explain . . . if there's anything I can do . . . '

'No, nothing,' she said hurriedly. 'But before my aunt comes down you'd better know what to expect.'

She told her story swiftly to the stranger. She had had to tell it so often to excuse poor Aunt Madge. Nearly twenty years ago Aunt Madge had lived happily here with her husband and her young son. Madge Cornell was of French extraction and her boy had been christened André after her father. Young André had been a brilliant musician. At his own request, he was sent to the Conservatoire in Paris to study. Then, all in the same week, two devastating blows were struck at Mrs Cornell's happiness. Her husband had been thrown from his horse, hunting. He died at once. Two days later she received news from Paris that her son had disappeared. Vanished and left no trace behind him. Nothing for his agonized mother but a note of farewell saying that he was sick of work and of life as he led it, and was going to South America with a friend — he did not say whom — to seek real adventure.

John Mostyn interrupted the story.

'Good lord! I come from South America. How strange! What made him go there? Why should he so suddenly chuck up his studies, and his home?'

'That is the unsolved mystery,' said

11

Lucy. 'It was generally thought among his friends that he was not the paragon my aunt imagined him, but just a weak, temperamental young fool who wanted to get away from parental authority. His father was rather strict. You see, the news never reached André about his father's death.'

'And he was never traced?'

'Never. But the double blow robbed my aunt of her reason. She isn't mad. She's sweet and kind and gentle. But she wanders a bit. I mean — every Christmas she thinks that André's coming back. Always we have a tree. But the candles are never lit. She says they must only be lit when André gets home.'

John Mostyn was silent a moment. He opened his lips to speak, but shut them again. He appeared to struggle with himself. Then, over his brown face came a queer, secretive look. He brought his attention back to Lucy. He thought it was very hard on this pretty girl that she should have to bear the load of sorrow in this deserted home.

She should have love and laughter, and a thousand candles lit before the shrine of her youth!

Then the door opened and Mrs Cornell came in, leaning on the arm of an elderly maid.

John Mostyn had never seen a lovelier old lady. Hers was a Dresden-china fragility of pink-and-white skin, of snowy curls, of forget-me-not blue eyes. In one hand she carried an ebony stick. Later he learned that she was not yet seventy. But years of suffering and of thwarted hope had aged her unbelievably. She might have been Lucy Cornell's grandmother instead of her aunt.

Lucy ran to her aunt.

'This is Mr Mostyn, darling. He's lost his way on the moors. His car has broken down. We can't let him go on in this snowstorm, can we?'

Mrs Cornell looked long and hard at the tall young man in the grey suit and tweed overcoat, who stood there twisting his hat in his fingers. She said, hesitatingly: 'André! André, isn't it you?

Haven't you come back so that we can light the Christmas-tree for you?'

He felt a sudden lump in his throat. He had adored his own mother and she was dead. Now, he was a hard-bitten man of the world with a bachelor flat in Rio, and he led a life that seemed a thing apart from this English home with its Christmas decorations. The sort of home he had heard about from his mother, who used to live in the Old Country, and which he had always wanted to have. He felt nothing but a strange desire to be very tender with the poor demented old lady who thought that he was her son.

'I'm so sorry,' he said. 'I'm not André. My name is John.'

Mrs Cornell gave a great sigh.

'Oh dear! Then I've made a mistake. You might have been André. You look a little like him, and he was about your age.'

'Darling,' said Lucy, feeling very uncomfortable. 'What shall we do? Mr Mostyn is stranded here.'

14

'He must stay, of course. He shall have dinner with us and he can have the spare room and welcome.'

'No, no,' began John Mostyn, 'I couldn't encroach on your hospitality. I'm a stranger to you.'

Mrs Cornell drew nearer to him, peering up into his face.

'Don't go,' she said wistfully. 'It's nice to have a young man in the house. André used to bring all his friends home, and now we have nobody . . . nobody . . . ' Then suddenly she began to weep. 'André, when will you come back? Oh, my son, my son!'

Lucy and the maid each took an arm of the old lady and led her out of the room. John Mostyn could hear her soft weeping and moaning as they took her up the stairs.

He walked to the window and looked out at the whirling snow. And under his breath he said: 'Good God! How strange! How more than strange. But I mustn't speak. I couldn't hurt her all over again.'

Lucy Cornell came back into the room.

'I must apologize. It was so embarrassing for you.'

'You needn't worry,' he said. 'And now I had better go.'

The dismay in her eyes was flattering.

'Oh, but don't. My aunt really means it. You must stay here the night. You can't possibly go on in this weather, on foot.'

'It's more than kind of you and your aunt — and very trusting. You know nothing whatsoever about me.'

The dimple reappeared at the corner of Lucy's mouth.

'Well, if you're a thief and you disappear in the night with the silver, you'll probably be found dead in a snowdrift at dawn, so it wouldn't do you any good.'

'That's true,' he said, and laughed. 'Well, I'm not a thief, I assure you.'

'I'm sure, too. Will you stay?'

'I think it would be marvellous,' he said.

They looked into each other's eyes. Suddenly, outside the door, there came the sound of childish treble voices singing:

'No-el! No-el! . . .
Born is the King of Israel.'

'The carol-singers!' said Lucy.

'How gorgeous,' said John Mostyn. 'I've wanted to hear something like that ever since I was a small boy. My mother used to describe the English Christmases. I used to dream of them in Rio. My father had a business out there, and I followed on. I've never seen England until now.'

'I'm afraid you'll find it very dull in this house.'

'Not if you're here,' he said impulsively.

Lucy was suddenly absurdly thrilled. And the thrill deepened when John Mostyn put his hand in his pocket, drew out half a crown and said: 'Let's give this to the carol-singers, shall we?'

She went with him to the front door feeling immeasurably glad that the stranger from South America had lost his way and come to Blakeley Grange. For he would be here tomorrow. And it was the first Christmas Eve that she could truly feel that there was something to look forward to.

Poor Cousin André had run away just before Christmas, all those years ago. So it was always at this time that Aunt Madge felt her Tragedy most. Consequently, the time which should have been the happiest was the very one which Lucy had grown to dread.

She began to think excitedly what fun it would be to have this gay and attractive young man to share Christmas dinner with Aunt Madge and herself tomorrow.

2

But that Christmas dinner was not destined to be for three at Blakeley Grange. Only for two.

On the night that John Mostyn found shelter at Blakeley Grange, Mrs Cornell was taken very ill. It was her heart, the doctor said when he arrived long after midnight after a twenty-mile drive. The poor tired heart, overloaded with suffering, had given way at last. He did not think that she would live until Boxing Day.

At first John Mostyn had anticipated leaving the Grange at once in the doctor's car, since he had the chance of a lift. But something in Lucy's brown eyes prevented him. A frightened appealing look. Poor pretty child! She would not want to be left alone with a dying aunt at this festive season. He would not go. He could not. And there were many reasons, apart from that, why he did not want to leave her. So the doctor went away alone. He promised to send a breakdown gang out from the garage in the morning to tow in John's car, which was by now half-buried in a snowdrift on the moor.

Lucy had never been more glad than when John elected to remain in the house. It was grand to have somebody to talk to whilst Florence nursed the old lady upstairs.

Lucy knew that it would be for the best if Aunt Madge passed beyond all suffering. If she lived, it could only mean protracted years of hopeless waiting for André. The son who must now be dead, otherwise he would surely have come back long ago.

'And what will you do once you're alone?' John asked Lucy as they sat before the fire which Florence had lit for them in the drawing-room.

'I don't know,' was her answer. 'It will seem so strange being on my own. But I think I shall want to travel; to see something of the world which I have always longed to do.'

'It's a crime that you should have been shut up here all these years.'

'One gets used to anything, and I read a lot and make all my own clothes. I ride, too. I love riding.'

'I'd like to ride with you one day,' he said. Then, looking down at her slender hands, added: 'And I bet you know how to handle a horse, too. You ought to ride with me in South America, up in the mountains where I have a ranch. You'd love the life out there.'

'Tell me about it,' she said.

So, sitting there in front of the fire, he told her a great deal about Rio, until she felt that she could see it all. Feel the drenching sunlight, the golden beauty of the loveliest harbour in the world. See herself in the mountains, upon a horse at the side of this tall young man, riding under the blue, burning skies. There was glamour in the thought. Glamour for her this Christmas Eve, in spite of The Tragedy which was drawing to its close upstairs. Glamour, when she realized that it was past two in the morning and that Christmas Day had come upon them unawares.

She and John Mostyn shook hands and said: 'Merry Christmas!' As though they were old friends. Then a little guiltily, Lucy said: 'But it won't be a very merry Christmas. I must remember poor darling Aunt Madge. Oh, if only she could have seen André before she died! That's what she keeps saying to Florence and me. 'If only I could see my boy. If only we could light the candles on the tree just once again.''

John Mostyn looked at the Christmas-tree in its dark, shadowy corner, then spread his hands to the blaze of the fire.

'She must have loved him very much.'

'She worshipped him.'

He, too, lifted his eyes to the ceiling and thought of the old lady who lay up there full of hope deferred and of bitter disappointment.

Then he looked back at the girl. Her

charming face was a little pinched and pale.

'Why not go to bed,' he said gently. 'You look tired, my dear.'

'My dear'! How naturally he said those words. How kind he was! And understanding. She thought that she could never have got through this night without him.

She refused to go to bed. She wanted to sit up and savour the strange sweetness of her new friendship with a man who had been but a stranger only eight hours ago.

He made her talk about herself and about her life here. Everything was centred around André. Upstairs was André's bedroom, with all his things just as he had left them before he disappeared. Every habit and custom connected with him had been carried out year after year by his mother. John Mostyn listened to the pathetic details. Heard about the chestnut mare, Polly, which André had ridden when he was on holiday and which had been specially cared for in the stables, nobody but the groom being allowed to ride her. About his favourite flowers, red roses, which all through the summer were put before his photograph which stood in his mother's bedroom. About the sweet home-cured ham he used to relish, and which was cured and cooked at this season. There seemed little that John Mostyn did not know about André by the time Lucy had finished her narrative.

And now she ended: 'It's all over. There won't be another Christmas here, not another tree decorated by me. The candles will never be lit. Never!'

'Who knows,' said John Mostyn strangely.

And again he cast his eyes upwards, thinking of the old lady up there.

It must have been just before the dark winter dawn broke that Christmas morning, that Florence, who had been up all night with her mistress, came running down to the drawing-room.

'Miss, please come. I'm afraid she's sinking.'

Lucy looked at John Mostyn. He saw that she was trembling. He took her hand and held it in a warm, tight clasp.

'Don't be afraid,' he said. 'I'll come with you if you like.'

She was glad of his presence and went with him up to the big bedroom which was dimly lit by fire-glow and a single lamp burning at the bedside.

Mrs Cornell looked at the two young people in the doorway. Her failing sight passed by the slender figure of the girl to the tall one of the young man. And suddenly she raised herself from the bed and whispered: 'So you've come! André, you've come!'

Lucy was about to move forward to voice the usual denial, when a strange thing happened. John Mostyn dropped her hand and ran forward and knelt beside the bed. He enfolded Mrs Cornell's tiny figure in the white shawl in his arms.

'Mother!' he said. 'Mother, darling!'

Lucy put a hand to her lips. She stared big-eyed at the two figures. She wondered if she was going crazy. This man, John Mostyn . . . *André*? And then came the gladdest sound she had ever heard. The sound of happiness in the lilt of Aunt Madge's voice. A voice grown peculiarly strong and clear.

'André! My son! *At last!*'

Lucy cupped her burning face with two shaking hands. She did not understand. She felt utterly bewildered. She could only stand there, transfixed, with old Florence peering behind her, bewildered in her turn.

'André, how long you've been in coming!' they heard Mrs Cornell say, and they could see her stroking the dark head of the young man which was laid against her shoulder.

'I'm sorry it's been so long, dear. You must forgive me.'

'It doesn't matter, now you're here. Nothing matters but that.'

'It's lovely to feel your arms around me again, Mother.'

'And yours around me. You're so strong, my son. You were always strong.

Do you remember how you used to lift me right up in your arms and call me *Petite Maman*? That was your father's name for me.'

'*Petite Maman*, yes. How are the horses, darling? Shall I be able to ride in the morning?'

'Of course you shall ride. There is a beautiful mare in the stable — your dear Polly's foal.'

'And the smoked Devon ham? Am I to have that?'

'It's downstairs, darling. Florence shall give it to you.'

Then Lucy saw her aunt kiss John Mostyn's forehead and heard her call: 'Lucy! Lucy! You don't know your cousin André. Come and make friends with him, my dear. Take him downstairs and show him your lovely Christmas-tree and light the candles, child. Light the candles! Isn't this what we've been waiting for? Isn't it? I knew André would come back on Christmas Day.'

Lucy came forward like one in a dream.

'Yes, Aunt Madge,' she said.

Then John Mostyn stood up.

'I'm going to put a blanket round you and carry you downstairs to see the tree lighted up, *Petite Maman*.'

Florence moved forward agitatedly and began: 'It'll kill her — and you are not — '

But Lucy interrupted: 'Hush! She's dying anyhow. Let her have just this . . .'

John Mostyn walked downstairs with that white sacred bundle in his arms. Lucy and Florence followed. There were tears in the eyes of both. Florence kept muttering: 'But it isn't him . . . I know it isn't . . . '

But Lucy said: 'Let her think so. Let her, Florence . . . '

It fell to Lucy's lot to light a wax taper and apply it to the candles on the tree. John stood gravely watching, with Mrs Cornell in his arms. The old lady was gasping for breath, but her face was radiant. And the radiance was intensified by the gleaming stars that winked out, one by one, from every little candle on that brave, tall tree. What a sight it was! How bravely the candles burned! The tinsel and the glass balls shimmered, and the silver star on the top took on an almost unearthly brilliance.

Mrs Cornell whispered: 'My son is home! Merry Christmas, my son!'

'Merry Christmas, Mother,' he whispered back, and kissed both her eyes. Eyes that suddenly grew dim as the white head fell back against his arm.

He turned and carried her out of the room. And Florence followed. But Lucy collapsed at the foot of the gay, shining tree, crying as though her heart would break.

When John Mostyn came down again, he lifted Lucy's prostrate figure from the floor and put her in a chair. He knelt beside her, chafing her cold hands gently with his.

'You mustn't cry, Lucy. She is so happy now. She died happy. Ecstatically so. You saw that for yourself.'

Lucy looked at him piteously through her tears.

'But you're not . . . ?'

'I'm not André, no. But I knew him, Lucy. I figured it all out once you began to tell me about him. And first of all I thought of breaking the news to you, then I felt it would be dreadful for her to know his end. To realize finally that he would never come back.'

'Then is he — ?'

'Dead. Yes. He got in with a rotten crowd out in Rio. He died in a drunken brawl over a Spanish girl in a café one night. I happened to be there. He was buried in a pauper's grave and nobody knew anything about him or bothered to trace his relatives. But I was one of the witnesses of his end, and I remembered his name, André Cornell.'

Lucy grew calm. The tears dried on her lashes. She clung to the warm, kind hands which were holding hers.

'That was a very beautiful thing for you to do. Knowing what you did — and to make her passing such a perfect one.'

'It was easy. You had told me so

much, I knew sufficient to play the part. You heard me. I felt I could not bear that she should die disappointed till the very end.'

Lucy looked at the tree which was still ablaze. The wax from the candles was dripping fast. They were nearly done.

'I never thought I'd see that tree lit up.'

'I'm glad you did,' he said gently. 'You're much too young and lovely to stay in the shadows.'

She gave a great sigh. 'Soon a new year will begin.'

'For you and for me. This night has forged a link between us, little Lucy. Shall I see you again? May I?'

She whispered: 'Yes.'

Then he leaned forward and kissed her hair and she no longer saw the shining tree, because tears were blinding her eyes again.

John Mostyn took her by the hand and led her to the window. He pulled back the curtains and raised the Venetian blinds. It was daylight, cold, grey, passionless. The garden was white, buried under the snow. From the distance came the chime of bells. Christmas bells, with their tidings of peace and goodwill.

In the sudden daylight the Christmas-tree paled. The last little candle burnt out. The smoke rose from it, in tiny spirals, like incense rising to heaven.

Love Matters Most

1

'Susan, you will meet the one-forty-eight from Victoria which gets into Crowley at two-fifty-two,' said Mrs Collishaw, in the tone of one who was used to being obeyed.

'I suppose I must,' said Susan, whose tone suggested that she obeyed only with reluctance.

'Don't be silly, darling,' said her mother. 'You know that John Blayde — '

'Is *Sir* John Blayde,' cut in Susan, with a set, not very sweet smile and a look of exasperation in her remarkably lovely eyes, 'has bags of gold, will almost certainly be an MP one day, has a manor-house in Leicestershire, and could give me everything I want. Yes, I know it all by heart, but it just doesn't interest me, my dear Mummy.'

Mrs Collishaw, drawing on suède gloves preparatory to going to a luncheon party, was hall-marked 'Society' in her fashionable, three-piece flowered silk, her black straw cloche hat on a grey, close-shingled head, and she looked more exasperated than her daughter.

Susan was a fool. Not stupid, no. She had brains and read too much and thought too much. But Mrs Collishaw really believed she would have preferred a more stupid girl who would, for instance, allow herself to be influenced by the thought of the worldly goods that Sir John Blayde could bestow upon her. Instead of which, she displayed no interest in the fact that one of London's most eligible bachelors was coming down here to meet her; and she never displayed any interest in any of the men who Mrs Collishaw considered 'good matches'.

Susan had what her mother called an out-of-date and overdone theory that romance should come first; that position does not count, but that desperate love on bread and cheese in a cottage (if one could find a cottage!) was preferable to a less desperate affair, which might start at St George's, Hanover Square, with a flourish of financial trumpets.

Fortunately, thought Mrs Collishaw, Susan had not yet met this prince of romance for whom she wished to ruin her life, but it was a continual nightmare to her mother, wondering when she might do so.

Mrs Collishaw swept in a blaze of glory and sunshine out of the house to her waiting car.

'Come along, dear, drive me to Lady Burstead's, and then come back and change and go to the station.'

Susan took her place at the wheel. She liked driving the car. She was glad that their chauffeur had gone. Until the new one came, Susan had to do all the driving. She much preferred it to putting on kid gloves and 'calling' with her mother.

Having deposited Mrs Collishaw on the neighbouring estate, Susan returned to Mulberry Court, had lunch alone, and considered the question of clothes.

She did not want to change and meet Sir John Blayde. She really wanted to take her two Cocker spaniels, get hold of the Blighe family, and go along to Ashley Woods for a picnic. And her mother loathed the Blighes because they were 'nothing and no one'. But Susan thought them good fun. She always liked simple, honest-to-god people. Since she had left school a year ago and been forced into a 'deb's' season she had rebelled. She intended to go on rebelling. Not for her mother or anyone else would she marry for money or position, or for anything but love.

She had never seen this Sir John. It was one of her godmother's little designs with Mummy — sending the noble baronet down here for the weekend. Of course he was Conservative, and Susan was supposed to be. But in her heart of hearts she leaned towards Socialism. But she didn't dare say so very often.

Susan Collishaw, twenty-one next birthday, would seem on the surface to have all that she wanted; being an only child, with a country home, a flat in Town during the winter, and a mother bent on furthering her position. But Susan was quite dissatisfied, and immensely lonely. She was, in fact, in one of her most depressed moods this afternoon when finally she set off to meet Sir John's train.

She knew her mother would never forgive her for keeping on the old linen dress. So she had put on a new grey tailor-made, and added the touches of extra lipstick, and nail-varnish and all that was expected of her. Reluctantly she left the two spaniels whimpering after her, instead of going to that picnic which she had wanted as much as they did.

It was quite a beautiful and fashionable Susan who walked on to the platform, with a large blue hat pulled over her bronze curls, two red roses pinned to the lapel of her coat, and blue suède gloves and bag in her hands. She just couldn't bear to put on those gloves, this warm June afternoon.

In came the train. Susan watched the people step out of it, her lips twisted into a faint, ironic smile.

'Poor Mummy's so transparent,' she thought. 'She needn't have lunched today with Eva Burstead. I expect she thinks Sir John and I will have a *nice* hour alone! I'm not sure she won't expect to find us in each other's arms when she gets back. Won't she be disappointed!'

Moodily she looked at the men who walked past her. How in heaven's name was she to recognize the weekend guest? She had never seen him, nor knew anything beyond the fact that her godmother, whose friend he was, had said he was tall and good-looking.

Then she saw a very tall and *very* good-looking young man in grey flannels, carrying a suitcase. Even the unimpressionable Susan found herself regarding this particular man with approval. He had the brownest face and the most handsome pair of hazel eyes she had ever seen. No hat and no gloves, and a rather casual air which appealed to her.

There were no other lone young men on the platform, so this *must* be godmother's choice, thought Susan, and moved forward.

'I'm Susan Collishaw from Mulberry Court,' she said.

The young man in grey flannels stopped, gave her an attractive smile and said: 'Ah yes. Mrs Collishaw said somebody would meet me.'

'How-do-you-do,' said Susan, and with some embarrassment extended her hand.

He looked equally embarrassed, but took the slender hand, and said gravely: 'How are you?'

'I've got the car outside,' said Susan. 'I'm doing chauffeur at the moment.'

'Well, let me drive now I'm here,' he said.

Susan stared. 'I wouldn't dream of it,'

she said. 'I adore driving.'

He put his suitcase in the back of the car.

'Where shall I sit?'

'Beside me,' she said, and took her place at the wheel.

'What a marvellous day!' he said, lifting his face to the sun and sniffing the pure fresh air appreciatively. 'After working in London it will be grand to be in the country, and I do love Sussex.'

'I agree with you,' said Susan. 'I loathe London and everything about it.'

'Do you really?' he said. 'Well, you don't know how much the country means to me.'

Susan thawed towards him. He was not only good-looking but fond of the country. That really was a change from most of the 'eligibles' Mummy produced — Londoners who either looked and behaved as though they spent most of their lives at cocktail-bars and in night-clubs dancing all night, or the frightfully hearty huntin' type, who could talk of nothing but horses and race meetings.

She turned the car out of the station-yard. They drove down the wide road that led to Mulberry Court, talking with some animation about the countryside.

Sir John was telling her that he had been born and brought up in the country. He seemed to know a lot about it. There was great excitement for Susan when they reached a crossroads on which stood a certain tree which had puzzled her for months. He knew at once what it was and told her so. That was very satisfying. And he knew a lot about cars, too. He disliked these big dignified cars as much as she did. They both agreed it was more fun to have a small sports car, open for preference, in weather like this.

She began to talk a lot, which was rare for Susan, she found it a thrill to be able to expound her particular views to someone who was in sympathy with them; someone whose main idea was not to discuss a week's gambling at Le Touquet, or bathing at Deauville, or

43

dancing at the Dorchester. Why, she could imagine Sir John might even like a picnic with herself and two spaniels and the Blighe family.

She said hopefully: 'Do you like picnics?'

'Love 'em!' he said. 'But I haven't had time for many lately.'

'Let's go for one tomorrow,' said Susan.

He looked down at her sun-tanned young face. What an amazing girl, he thought. She looked the last word in *Vogue* fashions, yet she was the most charmingly natural child. She enchanted him.

He stammered: 'Won't — won't Mrs Collishaw mind?'

'Heavens, no. Why should she?' said Susan, staring.

'Well, I must do some work — I mean — '

'Oh, you've not got to work this weekend,' broke in Susan. 'You've got to take a rest. I'm sure you need one. Ashley Woods are too marvellous. There's a lake close by. The Blighes have got a boat. Can you row?'

'Yes.'

'Then we'll go rowing,' said Susan.

And she felt as she had not felt for a very long time — that she was going to enjoy her weekend in the company of a young man of whom her mother approved. *What* a change!

At that precise moment the car choked, jerked, and petered out. Susan slipped the gear into neutral and pulled on the hand-brake.

'That's funny! She's got plenty of petrol.'

The young man jumped out of the car.

'Let's have a look.'

'Do you know much about the insides of cars?' asked Susan doubtfully. 'I don't.'

'Of course I do,' he laughed.

He whistled as he lifted the bonnet. The sunshine, the rich green pasture-land, the pale green of the oaks, the corn-fields and the flower-starred hedges were intoxicating to him. And so was Susan Collishaw, who looked at him with such dancing eyes, and was the most supremely natural person he had ever encountered. He began to think himself a little more than lucky.

He tinkered with the car for a moment and then looked up at Susan.

'I won't go into technical details because I daresay you won't understand, but we'll have to get her towed to a garage,' he said. 'It's something I'm afraid I can't do on the road.'

Susan descended.

'That's a bore. We're a mile from the Court. But we're only five minutes round the corner from Crawfords Garage. We'd better go and tell them to tow her in. And I've got a brilliant idea. It's such a marvellous afternoon — let's have tea at the Tudor House while Crawfords do the repairs. I'm so sick of home — and the Tudor House is the most darling little cottage where we can sit in the garden and eat homemade scones and honey.'

The young man looked down at her as though puzzled.

'Won't your mother — '

'Mother's out for the day,' broke in Susan, 'and I can do what I like — unless you're dying to get to Mulberry Court?'

'Not at all, but, Miss Collishaw — '

'Oh, I'm Susan to everybody. And must I go on calling you by your full and most noble title?'

He saw laughter in her eyes and dimples in the corner of her mouth, and his heart seemed to turn over. He would not have been human if he had not answered in the way he presumed she wished him to.

'I'd like you to call me Jack.'

'Then come on, Jack, and we'll walk to the garage, and here's where I become *myself*.'

Whereupon Susan, laughing, flung hat and gloves into the car, and with hands in her pockets and bronze curls bared to the sunshine, began to walk down the road beside the most delightful young man she had ever met.

2

'So you see,' said Susan, seriously, an hour later as she sat finishing her tea in the sunlit garden of the Tudor House, 'life's pretty difficult with a mother always wanting me to be a complete débutante and me always wanting to be just — myself. I feel you understand, don't you, Jack? You say you loathe Society as much as I do.'

'I do,' he said, 'my sympathies are entirely with you.'

'I'm awfully glad you came down,' said Susan, impulsively.

He looked across at her. There was no coquetry about Susan Collishaw. She was just utterly frank and much too attractive, he thought. He began to feel that this was all too good to be true, and that her attitude towards him could not possibly last. He had not the slightest wish to get to Mulberry Court and meet her mother. He would like to go on sitting here with her in this little garden, listening to her candid views and watching the varying expressions flit across her face. And he longed to tell her about himself. But that could wait for another day. He wanted to know much more about her.

The Susan who reached Mulberry Court later that afternoon, after the car had been repaired, was a very different girl from the one who had left it. She was no longer moody or depressed. She had found someone who *understood*. Someone who *agreed* that money was not half as important as friendship and affection. Someone who said he enjoyed a cup of tea in an old cottage much more than drinking a cocktail at the Ritz.

'You don't know how much I've enjoyed it,' he said, and a sudden flame leapt into his eyes that made Susan's heart miss a beat . . . a thing which had never happened to her in her life before. She felt almost as though she could not breathe. She turned quickly away from him.

'I've fallen in love,' she thought, deliriously. 'Gosh, I must be crazy, I've fallen in love at first sight. And I think he likes me, too.'

'Shall I put away the car for you?' asked Jack.

'No, thanks. I'll want it again to fetch my mother.'

'I'll do that.'

She turned and gave him a quick, shy smile.

'We'll both go.'

He swallowed hard. 'You're a darling,' he thought, 'but this won't do at all. It just — won't — do! If I don't keep my head I'll be fired from Mulberry Court before the evening's over.'

'Come on in and have a drink,' said Susan.

'But look here — '

'Is there anything else you'd rather do?' she asked, quickly.

She saw him redden slightly under his tan. Then meeting her gaze fully, he said: 'There's nothing I'd rather do.'

'Then come on,' she said gaily.

The butler approached.

'Madam has just 'phoned, Miss Susan, that Lady Burstead has asked her to stay on to dinner and would you mind entertaining Sir John?'

Susan could not resist a little giggle. More of Mummy's transparencies. But this time everything was just perfect. It would be great fun to dine alone with Jack. Tremendous fun!

'Did you hear that, Jack?' she asked.

He was lighting a cigarette. Through the smoke he smiled at her. 'What?'

'Mummy's staying out to dinner. Will you be bored dining with me alone?'

'But do you really want me to do that?'

Astonished, she answered: 'But, of course.'

'To be quite frank,' he said, 'I really don't know what to think of all this. I'm just walking on air.'

It was Susan's turn to change colour.

'I'm a bit up in the air myself. Well

— come on — let's have our drink. And let's do exactly as we want. I bet you loathe a boiled shirt.'

'I haven't got one — at least not down here.'

'Marvellous!' she said, starry-eyed, 'then stay as you are, and I'll stay as I am. We'll have our food as late as possible. In a few moments I want to drive you to Ashley Woods and show you my lake. It's lovely at sunset. Will you row me round?'

He shook his head at her.

'You're a most remarkable girl,' he said, not a little embarrassed. 'And I don't doubt your mother will be appalled — '

'But you're wrong,' said Susan. 'She'll be delighted. She got you down here, didn't she?'

'Yes, but — '

'And she told me to meet you and be awfully nice to you. So there you are!' Susan laughed, with cheeks aglow.

Entirely enslaved by her, he gave up protesting and followed her through the hall. And looking at the straight back and long, slim legs, he thought: 'She's completely adorable. I'm in love — I who never thought I'd fall in love for years! What a strange, mad, *marvellous* thing to have happened!'

The visit to Ashley Woods was a complete success. Jack took off his coat and rowed Susan over the pond which looked like a sheet of burnished gold in the setting sun. A magic mirror fringed with delicate alders and beech-trees that spread their foliage like green fans against the sky.

At first Susan and Jack talked at random about many things, then they said less, and gradually nothing. They just watched the changing sky — and each other. And in that hour the world changed for them both irrevocably.

They drove home in complete silence. But it was a silence of close contact. And it seemed to Susan that a miracle had come into her life — a miracle because she could *feel* this way about a man who yesterday had been a total stranger; a man whose arrival she had anticipated with boredom — even dread.

When they walked into the house it was Jack who spoke. He said: 'That was wonderful. One of the loveliest experiences of my life. But Susan, this must end.'

She put a hand to her throat. She thought:

'Now — is he going to tell me he's *married*, or something?'

But Jack had no time to tell her anything. Oxham, the butler, had arrived on the scene. He gave Jack a curious look, then said to Susan: 'I don't quite understand this, miss, but a call has just come through from Sir John Blayde's secretary. He says that Sir John was expected from Paris by 'plane this morning and had meant to come straight down here by train; but owing to urgent business he missed the 'plane and is now detained in Paris until tomorrow, which he much regrets.'

Susan stared. 'But, Oxham, you must have got that message wrong . . . '

'Wait,' interrupted Jack. 'I don't suppose he has got it wrong. I think I can explain.'

The butler gave Jack another look, raised his supercilious brows and departed.

Susan looked up at the young man. 'I don't understand.'

He said: 'Susan, I'm not Sir John Blayde. I knew that you'd made that mistake halfway through this afternoon. At first I admit I just thought you knew who I was and that you were being frightfully friendly, and I adored you for it. Then it struck me that you had been expecting somebody else, and I am afraid I let it go on. I let it go on because *I* wanted to go on seeing you, talking to you, watching you, even if, later, you turned me out of the place.'

Susan's heart almost stopped beating. She was a little white. She said: 'I still don't understand. Please come into the library and — tell me who you are.'

In the library he faced her with a look of deep concern on his handsome face.

'This is where I get the kicks. Susan, my name *is* Jack, and I'm not John Blayde. I'm just Jack Masters, the new chauffeur whom your mother engaged a few days ago. I think she must have forgotten to tell you I was coming by that train as well as Sir John.'

For a moment Susan could not speak. She was too utterly dismayed. Unbelievingly she stared at him. *The new chauffeur.* But it couldn't be true! He wasn't at all like an ordinary chauffeur. He was so cultured . . . and so . . . but Susan reproached herself . . . she mustn't think that way, that snobbish way, when all her life she had been against class distinction. She had made a very stupid mistake, and now that the whole truth began to dawn on her fully, the comic side seemed uppermost. She began to shake with helpless laughter. Covering her face with her hands, she laughed and laughed.

'It's so . . . terribly funny . . . ' she gasped. 'You . . . Mummy's new chauffeur. Oh, what a *gorgeous* mistake.'

Jack Masters said in a stiff, even injured voice: 'Yes, you can laugh. But it's not so funny for me. I've had a marvellous few hours with you and this is where my so-called job ends. The sooner I get back to London, the better. Goodbye, *Miss* Susan.'

Up shot Susan's curly head. Now he saw fear in her eyes. Breathlessly, she said: 'Oh no, you mustn't go, you can't.'

'My dear,' he said, 'how can I stay? It must have been obvious to you out there on that lake that I have fallen in love with you. A chauffeur can't be in love with his employer's daughter. That's why I am going.'

Then Susan cast discretion to the winds. She did exactly what her heart dictated. She said: 'But, Jack Masters — I don't care if you *are* the chauffeur. I wouldn't care if you were the sweep. I love you. I don't care whether you leave this job or not. You'll have to find another and take me with you, that's all.'

Across his face came a look of

complete bewilderment, then quite crazily he swept her into his arms. And Susan Collishaw was kissed as she had never been kissed before in her life, and as she knew she would not allow any other man on earth to kiss her.

At length, very tenderly, Jack Masters lifted her up into his arms, placed her in a chair, sat down on the arm of it and said:

'My darling, let's have cigarettes and that drink you once offered me. This wants a whole lot of talking over before your mother comes back.'

3

When Mrs Collishaw did come back she was in the company of her old and valued friend, Lady Burstead. Eva Burstead had insisted on driving dear Dorothy back to Mulberry Court, rather than allow her daughter to fetch her. And Mrs Collishaw insisted on darling Eva coming in 'for half an hour'.

'To meet Sir John Blayde, my dear. He's such an eligible young man! I do *hope* my naughty Susan has been making herself charming to him.'

The two ladies, entering the library at Mulberry Court, found Susan making herself very charming indeed to a tall young man in grey flannels. So charming that her mother blinked and gasped a little. For Susan was sitting on the sofa beside him, holding his hand, and they were looking at each other in a way which was quite unmistakable.

Mrs Collishaw fluttered forward with outstretched hand.

'Susan, *dear* . . . Sir John!'

'It isn't Sir John,' broke in Susan, jumping to her feet, and facing her mother with a flushed face.

'Not Sir John?' Mrs Collishaw's smile faded. 'Then who — ?'

'He's the new chauffeur, Mummy,' said Susan in an outrageously calm voice, 'and his name is Jack Masters.'

Mrs Collishaw went red and then pale. A shocked silence followed. She said icily:

'The new — *chauffeur?*'

Jack came forward. 'You'll remember engaging me,' he said. 'I was to come down to Mulberry this afternoon and you were going to have me met. Well, I owe you all sorts of apologies, but your daughter met me, and — '

'*Met you!*' Dorothy Collishaw broke in on a high note, and for a moment she looked and felt hysterical. She felt, also, the most burning shame. Susan had always been difficult. But *this* . . . this was monstrous. Good heavens! She *did* remember about the new chauffeur now. It had completely slipped her memory. She had been so full of plans about Sir John. And Susan had been holding the chauffeur's hand . . . *holding his hand* in the library . . . it was too much!

Trembling, Mrs Collishaw turned to her daughter.

'Are you out of your mind?'

'No,' said Susan. 'I may be a little crazy about Jack, but otherwise I'm quite normal. We've fallen in love and we're going to be married, and there you are.'

'I'm afraid it's true,' put in Jack gravely, and took Susan's hand back into his again.

Mrs Collishaw opened her lips to speak but closed them again. For once in her life words failed her. She did not know what to do next. To faint . . . to scream . . . to upbraid Susan . . . or to turn this outrageous young man out of the house.

And all in front of Eva Burstead. Eva who was the daughter of an earl, and the greatest scandal-monger in the neighbourhood.

The unhappy Mrs Collishaw turned to her friend. She was amazed to see no consternation on the face of Eva. In fact, Eva was having a quiet laugh to herself. And now she came forward and wagged a finger — yes *wagged* it — at the chauffeur.

'So this is what you've been up to all these weeks, Jack, is it? I wondered what you were doing. You always were an odd boy, but this is really the limit.'

Susan stared from Lady Burstead to Jack. 'Do you *know* each other?'

The young man drew in his lips. He looked thoroughly annoyed.

'Damn!' he swore gently under his breath, and added: 'Why in heavens name do I have to take a job and find you as a next-door neighbour, Aunt Eva?'

Mrs Collishaw pricked up her ears. '*Aunt* Eva!'

'Jack, what *is* this all about?' asked Susan.

'Darling,' he said, 'I've got myself into an awful muddle. But now the whole show has been given away. You see, I wanted you to go on thinking I was a chauffeur, because I thought we'd be so much happier living in a cottage, and me carrying on a job like that. Perhaps we could still do it, could we?'

Mrs Collishaw turned to her friend. 'Eva . . . is this . . . this young man your nephew?'

'He is,' said Lady Burstead grimly. 'Haven't you ever heard me speak of Jack? The intractable one of the family. Chauffeur indeed! He's the youngest son of my brother, Harry, ninth earl of Brenham. The Hon. John Masters, my dear. Masquerading as a chauffeur!'

'Not masquerading at all,' said Jack. 'I've been doing chauffeuring for the last six months *and* enjoying it. I got just as fed up with society as Susan. Just as sick of all the débutantes my mother hurled at me, hoping for the

63

best. And when I met Susan today I knew I had met the only girl in the world. Because she feels as I do about life. And what's more she was willing to marry me when she thought I was a penniless chauffeur, and that's enough for any man, isn't it?'

Mrs Collishaw broke into a beaming smile.

Really, she had had a frightful shock. But the youngest son of the ninth earl of Brenham . . . why she *couldn't* have chosen better than Susan had chosen for herself.

But Susan had burst into tears and run out of the room.

The Hon. John Masters followed her. He found her in the garden where it was growing dim, and the night-stocks and tobacco-plants were filling the air with summer fragrance.

He caught her up, gathered her into his arms and said: 'Susan, my little Susan . . . why are you running away from me?'

She sobbed on his shoulder. 'Because

I didn't want you to have a title or a position. I wanted you to be a chauffeur. I thought it was grand. It was simple and *real* and now it's all a dream that can't be true.'

'But why not, my sweet? What the devil does it matter whether I'm *me* or just Jack, the chauffeur? I love you and you love me. Surely it's love that matters most. All my life I've been trying to escape from the sort of life you hate. We needn't lead it. We can look for a cottage and a simple life together. And we needn't be married at St George's, Hanover Square, either. It can be in the village church. I don't mind, really, where we're married so long as we *are* — do you?'

Susan gave a long sigh and lifted her face to his. The first star in the blue summer sky was shining. But Jack saw only the shining of her eyes, and felt only the warm fervour of her young lips against his.

Later he whispered: 'Thank God, John Blayde missed that train, darling.'

Susan echoed: 'Thank God! You shall meet it tomorrow, Jack. You're still our chauffeur. You haven't got the sack yet, you know, darling.'

'I'd better try and keep the job. I'll never get another reference,' he laughed; and added with his lips against her curls: 'Don't let's go back to the house yet. Let's drive to the lake and I'll row you about in the moonlight, shall I?'

She gave him her hand. They walked in silence, utterly in love, towards the waiting car.

Some Are Born Wives . . .

1

When Charlotte married Bill she had a lovely wedding, just as she had had a lovely time all through her twenty-one years. Her father, retired from the Stock Exchange, was comparatively a rich man and he had always given Charlotte everything she wanted. More than anything in the world she wanted Bill Harrison. So she got him, because he was crazy about her, too, and there was nothing to stand in their way.

Bill was good-looking. Without being wealthy, he had adequate means, both parents having died before he was twenty-six, leaving him with eighteen hundred a year of his own, and every chance to make good in his profession as a barrister. He was clever. He had 'friends at Court' and by the time he met Charlotte he had already been briefed for one or two quite important cases.

They fell in love with each other at first sight at a cocktail party given by Lady Dewhurst, who was Charlotte's godmother, and whose son had been at Oxford with Bill.

It was one of those big parties held in a *bijou* house in Belgravia, during which all doors and windows were opened so that the crowd — and it was a crowd — could breathe. No one could move. Everybody talked loudly, drank generously, addressed each other as 'darling' and floated in and out of the little house leaving the hostess with little impression of whom she had or had not spoken to.

Charlotte was not fond of those sort of parties and she was bored until she met Bill. There was the usual circle of men around her, for she was extremely pretty and a good listener . . . then she saw Bill, very tall and square-shouldered and tanned from a recent holiday ski-ing in Wengen. When he turned and looked at her she thought she had never seen such blue eyes or such an enchanting schoolboy grin. It made him at once the most friendly and approachable person in the room. At that moment her godmother sailed across, swept Charlotte away from the man who was trying in vain to interest her in his peculiar woes and introduced her to Bill.

'This is my little god-daughter, Charlotte. Look after her, Bill.'

Bill Harrison, taking Charlotte's cool, slender hand in his, took a brief survey of the sweet grace and beauty of her — she wore black that afternoon with a short summer ermine coat and a little chiffon toque perched on a head that was wheaten fair. She had innocent eyes, of a smoky grey and just enough make-up to add a delicious touch of sophistication. Bill Harrison, a young man of innumerable affairs, nothing serious, of course, as he was enjoying his bachelorhood thoroughly, made up his mind then and there that he wished to take care of Charlotte for life. Neither of them talked to anyone else for the duration of that party. Four months later they were married.

The honeymoon was blissful. Charlotte and Bill were delighted with each other. They returned to London to the flat which they had taken in Lowndes Square, looking ridiculously proud and pleased. 'A perfect match,' it was called by those who knew them. They thought so. Charlotte was completely in love with her blue-eyed schoolboy of a husband, and he found the slender girl with the smoke-grey eyes who had drifted into his life at Barbara Dewhurst's cocktail party an enchanting wife. Not for a moment would he ever regret the surrender of his freedom.

Charlotte was not merely pretty, but intelligent. She could cook. She could sew. She was domesticated as well as touched by that glamour which made him want to take her out to dine and dance and introduce her to every man he knew, and say: 'This is my wife . . . '

They went out a lot. Charlotte adored dancing and Bill, for such a tall man, danced well and was an authority on jazz. Charlotte discovered that one of his minor accomplishments was being able to play, in quite a professional way, upon a saxophone.

That first year they were together brought them neither disillusionment nor ennui; they remained pleased with each other and the chic modern flat which they had furnished together. It was amusing and exciting picking up bits of furniture and china and just the things they wanted. Charlotte found a good maid — an Austrian girl who made them *Wiener Schnitzel* as it should be done, and huge cakes full of walnuts. They gave delightful little parties and everybody said how lucky and happy the Harrisons were and how much to be envied. At the end of such parties they retired to each other's arms feeling, indeed, inestimably fortunate.

The first Christmas of their marriage Bill took his annual holiday, and they went to St Moritz because he loved to ski. There he fell in love with Charlotte all over again. She looked so heavenly in her black ski-suit and gay woollens, and could skim over the snow with him as lightly and gracefully as a bird.

Then in the spring — about twelve months after their wedding — things changed a little. Charlotte found that she was going to have a baby. She was pleased because she had always liked children, and marriage, in her opinion, was incomplete without a child. But she did not feel very well, and those months of waiting dimmed her spirits and temporarily spoiled her looks. In those days Bill, awed by the thought of being made a parent and secretly proud, was more than ever tender and protective of his young wife.

In due course Charlotte went into the Lindo wing at St Mary's and produced her baby, having what the doctors and nurses called 'an easy time' although she did not think so, and to Bill, panicking while he waited, it was a nightmare.

The baby was a boy; nine pounds,

healthy, and a mixture of both parents, with Charlotte's daffodil head and his father's gentian eyes. Bill was terrified of him, but later, when he grew more used to his offspring, liked to hold and play with him. In due course he was christened Christopher after Charlotte's father and William John after Bill.

And now the necessity arose for making a change in the Harrison ménage. The flat in Lowndes Square, which was adequate for a young married couple, was not suitable with Christopher and his Nanny as additions. Charlotte's mother now stepped forward and asserted herself, as the 'one and only granny'. She belonged to the old-fashioned type of woman who did not think London healthy for babies. She told Bill that it was his duty to find a house in the country for Charlotte.

2

Reluctant to leave his flat and say goodbye to London life, Bill nevertheless obediently did his stuff, found an enchanting little cottage near Banbury, 'did it up' and moved his wife and son from the flat. Henceforth the Harrisons were to be seen no more at the cocktail parties, first nights and restaurants in Town.

Their new house was called The Thatched Cottage — unoriginal but descriptive. The little house — two labourers' dwellings knocked into one — had been built in the days of the Tudors. It had all the right things which made Charlotte and Bill start reading Beverley Nichols' *Down The Garden Path* again and appreciating it to the full. Oak-beams. Uneven yew floors. Bottle-glass windows. Funny little staircases. Unexpectedly big cupboards.

And an enchanting garden, which, with the help of a local gardener, soon yielded its complement of flowers and vegetables.

They had to start hunting for things all over again, finding old oak and pewter and *Famille Rose* china and the treasures essential to make The Thatched Cottage look 'just right'.

This time, Bill found himself very often having to go off in the car and hunt for antiques by himself. In fact, he had been a great deal by himself since the birth of Christopher. He did not notice the change in his personal life all at once. It came slowly, but bit by bit he saw less and less of his pretty wife. Somewhat to his astonishment, she was a most enthusiastic mother. Time and time again when he wanted her to go out with him or do something with him, he found her busy in the nursery with Nanny and Christopher and she would say: 'I'm so sorry, darling, but I must see Christopher have his bath . . . ' or 'I must finish making that little suit for Christopher . . . ' or 'I would have loved to have come but I've promised Nanny I'd take Christopher out in the pram while she does some washing . . . '

At first Bill made no protest. Although disappointed to be thus deprived of his wife's companionship, he respected this strong development of her maternal instinct and thought how lucky he was to have chosen a girl with so many attractions, who also made a perfect mother.

That was for the first year.

By the time Christopher was two, the Harrisons had settled down thoroughly to their rural existence and Bill went up to London every day. Sometimes — only when it was vital — if he happened to be working on a particularly strenuous case, he stayed a night in Town. The first time such a case occurred, he tried to persuade Charlotte to go up to Town and spend the night with him. But she was reluctant to leave home.

'I don't like being away from

Christopher,' she said.

'But there is Nanny,' Bill reminded her, 'and Josepha . . . ' (Josepha was the Austrian cook who was still their devoted maid.)

But Charlotte seemed to have the opinion that Nanny was not altogether to be trusted, and that Josepha was nervous in the country unless one of her employers was there. So Bill spent his night in Town alone. After doing this once or twice, he began to feel a natural irritation because he never now had the pleasure of taking his wife out. They hadn't danced at one of their old favourite haunts since Christopher was born.

He reminded Charlotte of this fact and impressed it on her that he was feeling neglected. Because she still loved him devotedly, she surrendered to his wishes and the next time he went to London for the night, she accompanied him, looking, as he told her, younger than ever and not at all like the mother of a big boy of two.

While they were at the hotel and

Charlotte was changing into an evening dress, a call came through from the cottage. Charlotte answered it.

Bill, shaving in the bathroom, heard her say: 'I'll dash straight back, Nanny. Yes, at once. I'll come by train.'

Bill came into the bedroom and saw Charlotte pulling off her evening-dress, looking white and anxious. She explained that Nanny had just called up to say Christopher had a temperature, so she was catching the first possible train back to Banbury.

'But, darling,' exclaimed Bill, 'small kids often run temperatures, don't they? Did Nanny say there was anything seriously wrong?'

'No, but I must go back.'

Bill's face went suddenly hard. 'I'm damned if I see why you should. If there's nothing very wrong except a slight temperature, it's probably some childish fever. He'll be as right as rain in the morning. We're going to dine and dance — you can't walk out on me like this.'

Charlotte gave him a shocked look and continued with her dressing, firmly planting a hat on her golden head.

'How can you be so heartless, Bill? I wouldn't dream of leaving Nanny to cope with Christopher if he's ill, and you ought to be the first to suggest me going back.'

'Well, I'm not,' said Bill. 'I think you are far too nervous about the boy. If you go on like this as he gets older, you'll make him soft. Besides, what the hell do we pay a nurse for if you can't leave anything to her? If you don't trust this one, get another whom you *can* trust.'

'Thank you,' said Charlotte icily, 'but I should never dream of leaving my child entirely to any nurse, and I'm horrified at you, Bill, for expecting me to stay and dance when Christopher is ill. Will you please 'phone down and ask them to send a boy up for my suitcase.'

He growled: 'Oh, hell, I'll take it down for you.'

He was thoroughly disappointed. He

had looked forward to this evening with his wife. He showed his displeasure by maintaining a stern silence while he drove with her to the station. Only a minute before the train went out he relented, and told himself that she was a damned fine little mother and that he oughtn't to be so selfish. So he asked her to kiss him and said he was sorry he couldn't go down with her, but he had to attend the Court so early in the morning, it wasn't worth while.

By now, Charlotte, resentful of his attitude and worrying about Christopher, had no smile for him and offered a cool cheek. The train went out. Bill returned to the hotel feeling thwarted and conscious of the first real rift in the lute between his wife and himself.

Charlotte got back to the cottage to find that Christopher's temperature was already down a little and that the nurse had been worried without any real reason. Once satisfied that her child was all right, Charlotte began to think about her husband again and regretted that she had refused to kiss him and that she had spoiled his evening. Incidentally she had spoiled her own, but she faced up to the fact that her child mattered enormously and that motherhood with her was a stronger tie than any of the rest.

3

Charlotte and Bill made it up, but the memory of that evening rankled with him. And there were other incidents during that summer that annoyed him equally.

When his next summer holiday came, he wanted to take the car and go over to France with Charlotte. They had had a rapturous honeymoon in Villefranche and he wanted to motor right along that coast and recapture with her the fervour of those first halcyon days.

But Charlotte would not go abroad and leave Christopher. In her opinion, she told Bill, once a couple had children, they should spend their holidays with them. Her mother had suggested that they should take Christopher to Saunton Sands in Devonshire. Charlotte wanted Bill to go to Saunton. There was a marvellous beach there and it

84

would be fun to buy Christopher his first bucket and spade and watch him paddle and take dozens of snapshots. And they wouldn't need Nanny. Charlotte would look after Christopher herself. Just the three of them. Didn't Bill think it would be heavenly?

Bill said '*M'm*'. But in his secret heart he hankered after the south of France and the casino, and dressing Charlotte up in lovely clothes and watching other fellows look at her and envy him. He reminded Charlotte that he hadn't had her to himself for two whole years. She was touched by his obvious devotion, but with the sweetest smile reminded him in turn that he was now a father and couldn't expect to be alone with her. *There were three of them — no longer two.*

Bill obediently went to Saunton Sands. He supposed that Charlotte was right and he wished he could be as fond a parent and as self-sacrificing. Not that he wasn't both proud of, and devoted to, his small son. In a way he enjoyed the holiday and took all the snapshots that Charlotte's heart desired, held his son's hand while he paddled, and built enormous castles on the beach. The days were all right but the nights, in his opinion, were ghastly. No casino. Nothing to do in an English seaside hotel but sit opposite Charlotte and read a book or be drawn into a game of bridge with some frightful old women who wouldn't play more than a penny a hundred. And he didn't see much of Charlotte, either, because she didn't like leaving Christopher alone in a hotel bedroom so she generally retired to bed soon after dinner. And when Bill joined her he had to undress in darkness for fear of waking his small son, whose cot was beside Charlotte's bed.

So life continued. If Bill had hoped that when Christopher grew older — and he was a strong little boy — Charlotte would be more available, he was wrong. For when Christopher was four, Charlotte produced her second child. A small girl whom they christened Susan, and who in contradiction to her brother was as dark as he was fair, with her father's dark curls and her mother's grave grey eyes.

Bill was delighted with his daughter. He admired her beauty and he thought it marvellous of Charlotte to give him such charming children. But gone now were all hopes of regaining the delightful companionship of the Charlotte whom he had first loved and married. She was now tremendously busy with both children and he seemed to see less and less of her. It was not that she denied him her love. On her own assurance she still wanted him for a lover as well as a husband. *But even when she lay in his arms these days, Bill had the deep and disturbing belief that she was no longer absolutely his. Even while her arms and her lips caressed him, she was still essentially the mother . . . still wondering if young Christopher's cut knee would heal without festering . . . or* listening subconsciously for Susan to cry . . . unable to eliminate that strong and potent side of her which belonged exclusively to them and which shut Bill right out.

4

After the Harrisons had been married seven years Bill reviewed his domestic situation and was bound to say that he found it disillusioning. The cottage was delightful. The garden had grown and matured. They had bought another field and a pony for Christopher. Josepha had returned to her native country and had been replaced by a married couple. Nanny was still in charge of the children, but Charlotte remained in charge of Nanny. And Charlotte was 75 per cent the mother these days and only 25 per cent the wife.

Bill had given up trying to take her away by herself. He had almost given up planning anything for Charlotte. She no longer seemed to care about parties or any of the amusements which they had once shared. She worried incessantly and unnecessarily about Christopher and Susan.

Bill loved his children but he did not always wish to be with them. Charlotte found it hard to accept an invitation which did not include them. People in the district knew it. It was a thorn in the flesh to various hostesses, especially during the summer months, that if they wanted Charlotte and 'that nice Mr Harrison who was so good-looking and such an asset to a tennis party', they must also ask the whole family.

One afternoon at such a party, the vicar's wife, eating an ice which Bill had dutifully brought her, remarked to him that 'little Mrs Harrison' was the ideal mother.

Bill agreed. He had just played three sets of excellent tennis and had almost forgotten that his wife was with him. He saw her at a table under the big oak-tree where tea was being served. She was holding a mug of milk to little Susan's lips. Christopher's high young voice saying: *Mummy* every five minutes echoed plainly through the chatter. Bill let his gaze rest a moment on his wife.

In his opinion for a long time now, she had lost her old glamour. The slender girl whom he had loved so passionately was still pretty — she could never be anything else with her lovely eyes — but her hips had broadened. She was definitely plump, even matronly. Her shining hair was untidy. She had given up smart clothes and, more often than not, wore 'sensible' slacks and jerseys. Today she looked flushed and a little anxious-eyed, as usual when she tended her children. She had no time for anybody else. Bill wondered gloomily what she would do in a year's time when Christopher went to prep. school. She seemed to dread parting with him. He supposed that she would then engross herself in Susan.

'So wonderful with her needle,' the vicar's wife was murmuring in Bill's ear, 'I believe she makes every stitch your small daughter wears and she is always turned out so exquisitely. You are lucky, Mr Harrison.'

Politely Bill agreed. But in himself he could not agree. *For he knew that first and foremost he wished that Charlotte had been an ideal wife. She did not seem to be able to balance the two sides of herself equally. The scales weighed down always on the side of the children.*

Despite the fact that he had almost given up appealing to her to give him more of her attention, a restless, even resentful mood seized him that night, and when they were alone in their bedroom, he asked her to go away with him for a long weekend.

'I'm in the mood for a gamble and a little excitement. We'll fly to Monte Carlo and spend an extravagant day or two at the Hermitage. You can get yourself a new evening dress. Come on, Charlotte . . . let's beat it up like we used to, eh?'

Charlotte, rubbing a little grease into a nose which she had allowed to peel unbecomingly through too much sun, turned and smiled at her husband. He knew that smile — friendly but elusive.

'Darling, it sounds grand, but I couldn't possibly.'

'Why not?' he asked.

'Well, you know that Nanny has gone and I don't altogether trust this new girl with Susan, and — '

'Now look here, Charlotte,' broke in Bill, 'don't be damned ridiculous. You never trusted Nanny, and now if you've got a girl you can't trust you'll remain tied as usual to the kids. Get your mother to come down here and stay while we're away if you haven't any faith in the new girl.'

Charlotte turned away from him and continued creaming her face.

'I've no intention of asking my mother to do what is *my* duty.'

Bill lost his temper, suddenly and quite violently, for the first time in the seven years of their marriage.

'And what about your duty to *me*? How do I come off in this show? I'm fond of the kids, but, damn it, have I a wife or haven't I? I'm just about sick of this stuff you put over about the children. You're overdoing it. I tell you, Charlotte, you're driving me too far, and you'll be sorry for it one day.'

Charlotte dropped the cream-pot and stood up. She looked white and startled. He could see that he had frightened her, wounded her deeply, and that she did not understand what lay behind his outburst. She exclaimed: '*Bill!*'

'Well, I mean it. Everything is for the kids, morning, noon and night. *You're such a damned fine mother that you make a damned bad wife* and you might as well know it — ' He broke off.

A moment's silence, then Charlotte said: 'I'm sorry if that's how you feel. I didn't think any man in the world would shout at his wife because she is a good mother.'

He gritted his teeth. 'Can't you understand, Charlotte?'

'I understand that you are jealous

because I look after Christopher and Susan and won't leave them . . . which I consider right while they are little. Nothing that you can say will alter me, but I shall never forgive you for being so selfish and cruel about it.'

He looked at her speechlessly, then turned and walked out of the room.

That night Bill slept in his dressing-room. The scene was not referred to by either of them in the morning. But the incident marked the beginning of a new phase between them. A phase in which they ceased to be lovers. And if Charlotte was unhappy about Bill and the sudden breach, she did not show it. More than ever she interested herself in her children.

5

Bill went to the South of France.

While he was away Charlotte telephoned to her mother. She told her what had happened and added:

'Perhaps I've been wrong, Mummy. Perhaps I ought to go away with Bill and leave the children more. But I just can't. I'm always so afraid that something will happen to them.'

Mrs Greene upheld her daughter. She was a cold creature. She had married Charlotte's father never having experienced the *grande passion*, and like so many women had accepted her husband in a passive way, and poured out her heart on her young family. Charlotte and her two brothers had always counted before the unfortunate Mr Greene.

'You are absolutely right, darling,' she comforted Charlotte, 'and I'm very surprised at Bill for feeling as he does.'

'I'm miserable about it, but it can't be helped,' said Charlotte.

In Monte Carlo Bill was one of a party which included Katherine Cornelian. She was a young American woman about his own age, who had recently divorced her husband and was wandering about the Continent at a loose end. She was the antithesis of Charlotte. Tall, on the thin side, with the long, beautiful legs of the American. She had a sleek, dark head, a golden skin and a large laughing mouth. She was perfectly made-up and perfectly dressed. She was hard. Her eyes shone with a diamond-like brilliance, but she had a wit and a certain understanding of men which 'got' Bill from the moment he was introduced to her. Katherine liked the handsome English barrister, and within half an hour of talking to him she discovered the fact that he was not too happy at home. 'Family-ridden' she called it. Obviously blessed with one of those *dear little wives*, who unwisely exchange the allure of a French perfume for the violet odour of baby talcum-powder. What a mistake!

Katherine decided that she would like to have an affair with Bill Harrison. She set herself out to attract him. She gave him all the sympathy he was in need of, and when Katherine concentrated on a man she did not spare herself. She played tennis as well as Bill. She danced beautifully. During that long weekend Bill found himself inseparable from the tall, amusing, American girl. And those long golden legs of hers — and there was plenty of them to be seen when she wore her white shorts on the tennis court — were poems. Her wit dazzled him and she made him laugh. She liked to be with him and showed it. For a long time now he had been living with a woman who liked to be with him only when the children didn't want her, and then with an eye and an ear on the nursery.

Bill had loved Charlotte desperately once. He did not want to be unfaithful to her. It was the last thing he had ever meant should happen, but he had an affair with Katherine Cornelian. That weekend roused him out of the apathy and indifference with which he had lately regarded life. He returned to England frankly facing the fact that Charlotte and her mother-complex bored him stiff.

He went on seeing Katherine.

At first he felt guilty and ashamed of himself. He bought Charlotte a new diamond clip for which she thanked him charmingly. But there seemed no opportunity for her to wear it. It wasn't suitable for The Thatched Cottage and she never now allowed herself a night in Town.

Gradually, as the months went by, Bill settled down to an almost platonic existence with Charlotte. And his feeling of guilt diminished. He gave Katherine some beautiful earrings and had the pleasure of seeing her wear them when they dined and danced together in Town.

Katherine knew a great deal by now about Charlotte Harrison.

'I feel an awful worm when I see her with those kids and realize how good she is, and how some women neglect the family and just beat it up,' Bill told Katherine one night, in a mood of depression.

She knew these moments when 'conscience' pricked Bill, and gave him her most engaging smile.

'Don't let it get you down, honey. I've no doubt Charlotte is a good woman through and through, and a swell mother, but she's failed *you*. I can't forgive her for that and I don't see why you should.'

'She doesn't think she has failed me,' said Bill.

'Well, I'm sorry for her,' said Katherine. 'She's been such a sap. You were worth keeping. However *I'm* not complaining. Charlotte's loss is my gain.'

He looked at her searchingly.

'Do you really care for me, Kathy?'

'You know I do.'

'Well, I can't go on as I am. I don't feel it's fair on Charlotte — or myself — or you. If I break away, Kathy, will you marry me?'

Her hard, brilliant face softened a little. 'You won't have to ask me more than once, Billy-boy.'

He gave a sudden hard laugh. 'You won't want a family, will you?'

'No sir!' she said. 'I'm the reverse of Charlotte. I don't have the mother instinct. But I swear I'll make a peach of a wife.'

Bill went home and told Charlotte that he had met somebody else and that he wanted a divorce.

She received the news in silence, but the grey eyes she raised to his were so full of shocked surprise that he felt almost a murderer. He had stiffened his purpose to carry this thing through by telling himself that Charlotte wouldn't mind. Yet here she was looking at him with those stricken eyes and he felt a cur.

'I'm terribly sorry, Charlotte,' he said, 'but you will admit that we haven't seen eye to eye for a long time, and you'll have the kids of course. After all, you don't see much of me now — you're always with them — it won't make much difference if I don't come home at night and hang my hat up in the hall.'

Charlotte remained speechless. It was Sunday — the one morning on which she allowed the nurse to give Christopher and Susan their breakfast while she had hers in bed. She had been reading the paper when Bill came in to see her, and she had wondered why he was dressed for Town instead of in the old grey flannels which he wore when he was lazing about in the garden. He was going up to London. He had already packed. He was going away and never coming back. *He had found somebody else.* There was another woman in his life.

Bill turned away from her and looked out of the window down into the garden. He saw Christopher pedalling a tricycle down the path and little Susan running after him. Bill felt a pang, for these were his children and he was fond of them. From now on he would only see them occasionally. But Katherine, who was so completely engrossed in him, Katherine would give him everything else that Charlotte had not given except for a short time before the children were born.

He turned back to Charlotte and said: 'I daresay I'm to blame. Perhaps I never was a family man at heart. Anyhow I'll take the blame if that will make you feel better. But you must admit that with you it has been everything for the kids. I am just not prepared to take second place for the rest of my life.'

Then Charlotte spoke. 'I don't understand. I thought you loved the children, too.'

'I did, Charlotte — I do. But I don't want to sacrifice everything to them. For years now you haven't taken a holiday alone with me. You haven't let up on this mother-stunt for a second. I am always taking second place. I can't stand it any more.'

She clasped her hands together with a gesture which was both bewildered and pathetic.

'But I don't understand,' she reiterated. 'I've tried to do my duty to both you and the children.'

'No,' said Bill. 'To them — yes. To me — no. I think you did at first. We used to be very happy, but gradually I've been shoved into the background. Now I've found somebody who wants me. I'm sorry, Charlotte, but there it is. You must let me go.'

She covered her face with her hands.

'I think it is the cruellest thing that ever happened,' she whispered. 'If I'd neglected my children, you would have preferred it.'

'No, my dear, that's an exaggeration, but I admit I would have preferred not to be entirely neglected myself.'

Another silence during which Charlotte struggled with herself and her emotions. She could not begin to count the cost of what she had lost at the moment, nor, indeed, did she understand why she had lost it. It just seemed to her iniquitous that any man should wish to be placed in front of his own children.

'Oh,' she said at length, 'I don't deserve this . . . I know I don't.'

He looked at her with pity. 'Poor Charlotte, I'm sure you don't in your own mind. And as I told you at first, I am willing to take all the blame.'

A shriek went up from the garden. A piercing cry followed by a storm of weeping. Christopher's voice shrilled up at his mother's window: 'Mumm-ee, oh, Mumm-ee. Sue's fallen off my bike and cut her knee.'

Up jumped Charlotte. The tears were pouring down her cheeks but she brushed them away, slid into bedroom slippers and a dressing-gown and called to her son: 'All right, darling, Mummy's coming.'

She ran out of the room. Bill stood at

the window and watched. He saw Charlotte fly to his small daughter and snatch her up in her arms and caress the hurt knee. He heard her voice.

'There, my pet, there! Did you hurt your poor ickle knee. Mummy will put something on it. Come along, don't cry, angel.'

Bill Harrison walked into his bedroom, shut and locked his suitcases. He knew now that there could be no turning back.

He believed that in her way Charlotte still cared for him, and that she was terribly hurt, and that for a time she would miss him. But it had been typical of her that even in this moment when she knew that she was losing him, Susan's trifling hurts had mattered more than his — even more than her own!

He remembered something that Katherine had said to him, last night: '*Some women are born wives, and some are born mothers. I suppose the happy medium is the ideal.*'

Well, he hadn't found that ideal, and now he didn't want it. He only wanted Katherine who was obviously a born wife.

Charlotte lunched alone with her little family. Christopher had a big appetite. He ate up everything. Susan had to be coaxed a little. She kept her mother busy making her eat her vegetable purée which Charlotte herself always put through the sieve, because she was not sure the cook did it properly.

Charlotte ate no lunch. An hour ago Bill had driven away in his car, and he was never coming back. There would be no 'hanging up his hat in the hall' tonight or any other night. He was going straight to his other woman — an American. He intended to marry her as soon as he was free.

It wasn't until lunch was over and the children were taking their afternoon rest that Charlotte really had time to sit down and think things out. And the more she thought, the more her heart sank, and the more conscious she became of failure. Failure as a wife, although as a mother she was so completely triumphant.

She had lost Bill. She could scarcely believe it. Despite their recent estrangement, she had never for an instant imagined that she would lose him. She had never been jealous of him. She had taken for granted the fact that he was her husband just as he was the father of Christopher and Susan, and belonged here in The Thatched Cottage with all of them.

But he had gone. Because he hadn't liked 'playing second fiddle' to his own children.

In Charlotte's bemused and unhappy mind she could not comprehend that side of Bill. For in herself she was willing at all times to be of secondary consideration to Christopher and Susan. She would have liked it even if Bill had given them all his time. She supposed she had made a mistake in thinking he could look after himself. She should have treated him not merely as a husband and a father, but also as a child . . . one of the children who continually called upon her for sympathy, for love, for attention.

Now he had gone to some other woman for those things.

Charlotte lay face downward on her bed and faced the fact that it was not Bill who had smashed up her life, but she who had smashed up her own. She wondered how she was going to bear it.

The nurse knocked on the door.

'Are you taking the children to Mrs Wallace's for tea, or am I, madam? You know it's Diana Wallace's birthday party.'

Charlotte said: 'You take them. Tell Mrs Wallace I am not well.'

The nurse said in a tone of some surprise: 'All right, madam.'

Charlotte pressed her face into the pillow and thought: 'Bill . . . I want Bill back . . . oh, what am I going to do?'

She remembered what he had said to her this morning: '*You'll have the kids.*

*After all you don't see much of me now
— you're always with them — it won't
make much difference . . .* '

She knew that it would. He had
always been there in the background.
Without that background there was no
real foundation for her existence —
even with the children.

For the rest of that afternoon she felt
half-demented. She could get hold of
Bill tomorrow in his chambers. He had
told her that any time she wanted him
he would be there. She contemplated
telling him in the morning that he must
come back and that she wouldn't give
him a divorce; no, she would never set
him free; would never let the children's
father marry another woman.

She alternated between plans that
were spiteful and pathetic and ended by
experiencing a crushing sense of defeat.
She decided that it would be more
dignified to let Bill go.

And then nurse brought Christopher
and Susan back from the party. Nurse
looked scared and Christopher was

crying. He had been sick — it wasn't what he had eaten, nurse said, because he had refused his tea, but he had a pain. Mrs Wallace thought it might be appendix.

Charlotte forgot Bill. Charlotte panicked about her son, and in a measure was lifted from suicidal misery into action and the joys of service again. She telephoned to the doctor and put Christopher to bed. She fussed around with hot water, thermometer and crushed aspirin to relieve the little boy's pain.

Bill must go his own way. Why bother to love a man anyhow. All men were selfish brutes.. The only satisfaction women really got out of life was through her children.

Some women are born mothers . . .

Thanks for the Memory

1

There it was in the morning paper for all the world to see. For Dinah, herself, to see. Dinah who opened the paper with trembling fingers dreading to find what she knew would be there, since her mother had inserted it. Wondering desperately how it had ever happened . . . how such an announcement could possibly be . . . remembering with a pain in her heart almost too great to be borne, that other morning four months ago when she had rushed downstairs to breakfast, because her mother had said:

'Look . . . what a thrill, darling. Your engagement notice is in . . . '

And she had looked . . . and it had been a rapture, the very antithesis of this misery which enveloped her like a black cloud today.

Mr and Mrs Willis exchanged unhappy glances. Simultaneously they glanced at their only daughter, miserable for her sake, wishing that Pat Delaney had never come into her life. For it was Pat who had broken the engagement a week ago.

Dinah's fair head dropped over the paper. The next moment her parents saw the tears drip on to the printed sheets. It was too much for Mrs Willis. She sprang up and folded the slim quivering figure in her embrace.

'Oh, my darling, don't let it get you down. Be brave, be proud, darling. He's behaved like a cad. Don't grieve for him. He isn't worth grieving for. You're only twenty-one, darling, at the beginning of your life . . . and there are heaps of other men . . . half a dozen who would come round now if you telephoned.'

Dinah dropped the paper and gently, but firmly, disengaged herself from her mother's embrace. She was crying bitterly, without any pride at all. Her white young face was a mask of misery. Between clenched teeth she said: 'I wouldn't care if twenty thousand men were willing to come round. I don't want them. I loved Pat. I *adored* him. Oh why, *why* did this ever happen to me?'

Mr Willis rose from the table. He was embarrassed by this display of emotion, but deeply sorry for his daughter. He wanted to go round to young Delaney's flat and thrash him. The young scoundrel. The young whippersnapper, throwing up his lovely Dinah and only a month before their marriage, too. They had arranged it for the end of March.

Mr Willis advanced towards Dinah.

'I'll see Pat,' he said gruffly. 'I'll *make* him come back if you feel as badly as this about it, my darling.'

Then the tears dried in Dinah's lashes. (How often, she thought desolately, Pat had kissed those lashes and told her they were long enough to curl around his heart.) He had been awfully good at saying things like that in his beguiling Irish way. She could think of a dozen things he had said about her eyes being like the blue lakes of

Connemara and her lips redder and lovelier than the cardinal flower, every curve of her designed for man's loving. For *his* loving in particular.

Said Dinah: 'Don't dare suggest such a thing, Daddy. Pat has asked to be released. It's finished, *finished*! I'd die rather than let him think I wanted him back. Oh, but I wish I were dead!'

She turned and rushed out of the room.

Her parents nodded to each other.

'Get her away,' said Mr Willis. 'Get her away as soon as you can. That's the thing. We are facing bad times, but we are not poor yet. I can give you the cash, my dear. Take her on a cruise or get her out to Italy. She'll meet plenty of new fancies out there. She won't break her heart for ever.'

And Mrs Willis, with a handkerchief to her eyes, murmured: 'It's to be hoped not, poor darling. But unfortunately our Dinah has a very loyal nature. It'll take her a long time to get over this calamity.'

Upstairs in her bedroom, Dinah Willis lay face-downwards on her bed and sobbed. Just as she had sobbed for the last week. She wondered if she had any tears left. But ever since Pat sent that awful, unexpected letter, saying goodbye, she had been crying. She had scarcely eaten, scarcely slept. She was looking a wreck. Her radiance, her colour, the laughter which usually came so easily to her lips had all gone. She had loved Pat with all her soul, and the worst of it was she loved him still, even although he had broken her into pieces. If only she knew why he had done it! They had been so happy together. He had sworn a thousand times that she was the only girl in the world for him and the only one he had wanted to marry. They had lived in an enchanted world during their engagement. A world built up of breathless kisses, the poignancy of the shared embrace, the gaiety of the jokes over which they laughed together, the magical dreams of their future. It had been perfect. They had seemed perfectly matched. Even their financial prospects had been rosy. Dinah had a small allowance of her own and Pat, although but twenty-seven, held a good position in an engineering firm in London.

The last time she had seen him (a week ago — but it seemed to Dinah a hundred years) she remembered that he had appeared to be a bit subdued. He had come round to fetch her for a walk. They liked to walk down by the river — marvellously happy together — even on the chilly nights of early spring. Pat with a pipe in the corner of his mouth; those handsome eyes of his turning continually in her direction; she with a hand tightly locked in his.

But that last time he had hardly laughed. And when he had kissed her good night, it had been with a queer kind of desperation. After that the letter. Just the most cruel thing that had ever been written. The hardest words . . . and from Pat, whom she had thought could never be anything but tender and considerate.

★ ★ ★

Forgive me, Dinah, but I find that I can't marry you and that it is best for us to say goodbye. All I ask is that you'll forget me and please, don't try to get in touch with me because it would be more than I could stand.

Pat.

From the hour she had read that letter, Dinah had been sunk. At first she had felt a frenzied desire to telephone the office or ring up his flat; then pride had forbidden her to do so. Not only because he had asked her not to get in touch with him but because she must not cheapen herself. Pat said he had made a mistake. Pat did not wish to marry her, so it was not for her to plead with him.

But oh God! she thought this morning, as she lay sobbing against her pillow, how hard it was to bear. Not even to know what had made him change his mind. Left to guess, miserably, a dozen reasons. Perhaps she had loved him too much and he had grown tired of her ... perhaps there was another woman. Pat had an Irish devil in him and an eye for a lovely girl. Perhaps ... but she couldn't go on wondering. Her mind hurt, her thoughts would tear round in a vicious circle.

It had all happened a week ago since when she had not seen him, and had only heard from him once. That was when he acknowledged the engagement ring which she had sent back to him — and returned it to her. He wished her to keep it, he said. She had kept it. She had locked it away in her jewel-case and could not even bear to look at it. Her mother had taken his photograph away from her bedroom ... and the little travelling-clock he had given her on her birthday ... anything that could remind her of him. Poor Mummy, trying to be tactful! But Dinah needed nothing to remind her of Pat. He was there, ever there with her. Try as she would, she could not tear him out of her heart.

Through the wall came the droning sound of a radio. The people in the flat next door played their radio all day. A gramophone record . . . Dinah instantly recognized the old tune and it was like another knife being turned in her heart! 'Thanks for the Memory!'

She and Pat used to call that their signature tune. They had treasured every memory of each other. But there had been tragedy in the song for Dinah then. '*How lovely it was!*' she used to whisper to him, and he would answer:

'How lovely it is *going to be*, darling.'

Dinah's small clenched fists beat against the pillow.

'Oh, Pat!' she whispered. 'Pat!'

And then put the clenched fists against her ears to shut out the music from next door.

2

About a fortnight later, Dinah stood with her mother on the deck of a small liner bound for the Mediterranean. A Dinah who nursed a broken heart a little more bravely and who had a smiling mask for the world. A Dinah who tried to appear pleased and grateful because Mummy had given her some lovely new dresses, and here they were, going on a trip which, in former days, would have thrilled her beyond measure. Mummy was being so kind, Dinah hadn't the heart to let her see what it cost her to leave England. To leave Pat, and to have to say with a cynical twist of the lips and the bitterest meaning: 'Thanks for the Memory.'

It was a brisk March day. As the boat moved out, Dinah looked at the grey choppy water and tried to anticipate with pleasure what was awaiting her.

She would see Gibraltar, Malta, the hot sun and the blue skies of Italy. She would have the chance to forget.

'Only I never can,' said Dinah to herself.

Mrs Willis said: 'Well, now we're off, darling. Let's go down to our cabins and unpack.'

Dinah nodded. With apathy she walked through the crowds on the deck. One or two young men turned to look at her twice. Dinah was always a figure to be looked at, with her slenderness, her fair lovely little head and eyes even more beautiful than they used to be, perhaps because of the very sorrow that had deepened them.

But Dinah saw nothing and nobody. Down in her cabin, which she was to share with her mother, she picked up a passenger-list.

'I wonder if we know anybody on board?' she said.

'Perhaps there will be someone nice,' said Mrs Willis brightly, and started to arrange the carnations which Mr Willis had sent, and to glance again through some of the telegrams from relations and friends wishing them *bon voyage*.

Dinah glanced indifferently through the list. Then suddenly she uttered a cry which made her mother drop the carnations and swing round in consternation. She saw Dinah staring at the passenger-list looking as white as a ghost.

'Darling, what is it?'

Dinah said in a hollow voice:

'My *God*! Pat's on board.'

'Impossible!'

Dinah pointed to a name with a slender shaking finger. Her mother read it with mingled feelings of dismay and anger. Yes, sure enough there was that name. *Mr P. G. Delaney* . . . Malta. Dinah dropped the list and stood up. She said: 'Of all the catastrophes, and why in heaven's name is he going to Malta?'

Mrs Willis spread out her hands. 'I can't think. And I brought you on this trip to help you put him out of your mind. This is really *too* much!'

It was Mrs Willis who dissolved into tears, not Dinah. Dinah felt rather cold and hard. She said:

'Don't bother, Mummy. I'll deal with him. I feel quite able to. It is the most unfortunate coincidence that he should be on board this boat, but we'll get over it. I don't suppose for a moment that he realizes I'm here. He'll probably be just as embarrassed as I am.'

'Oh darling!' groaned her mother, 'don't let this upset you all over again.'

'I won't allow it to, believe me,' said Dinah. 'Cheer up, Mum, and let's go on with our unpacking.'

But even as she spoke, Dinah's heart was knocking. Pat on board . . . for twelve days, until they reached Malta. They must inevitably see each other, meet each other. It was going to be a strain.

But Dinah had got herself in hand, and pride was very much to the fore when she first came face to face with the man to whom she had once been engaged.

They met on deck just before tea.

Dinah in a tweed coat, fair curls blowing to the wind, was taking a brisk constitutional alone. Pat Delaney seemed to be doing the same thing. He came striding along the deck with the agile walk so familiar to her and his all-too familiar pipe stuck between his teeth. Handsome, heartbreaking Pat, with his black head and his square chin. Dinah tried to walk past him but it was not to be done. They stopped face to face. Pat swept the pipe from his mouth. For a moment they stared at each other. A blank, awful stare, as between strangers. Then Pat said: 'I want you to know that I had no idea that you were on this ship when I booked my passage.'

'Please don't apologize,' said Dinah in an icy little voice, 'and I assure you that my mother and I did not know that you were travelling on this boat, either.'

Silence. The big ship ploughed its way through the water leaving a long line of white foam behind it. Darkness was falling and there were lights glowing from every porthole. A gramophone was being played in the saloon where tea was served. A young couple, arm in arm, passed Pat and Dinah laughing gaily. And Pat and Dinah just stood there looking at each other with that awful strangeness which hurt Dinah to the soul.

Pat seemed utterly nonplussed, yet he could not move on. He said: 'I . . . I saw your name on the list.'

'We saw yours.'

'You . . . are doing the whole cruise?'

'Yes.'

'You ought to like it. It will be lovely at this time of the year.'

'Lovely, I'm sure,' said Dinah.

Pat Delaney stuck the pipe back between his teeth.

'No doubt I'll see something of you during the voyage,' he said desperately.

Dinah bit hard at her lip.

'Wouldn't it be more sensible if we forgot that we knew each other?'

Pat dragged his gaze from her. He was thinking how ill she looked, and how unutterable it was of fate to have done this thing to them. He had so hoped he would not see her again. He could not bear to see her. If she knew how he longed to catch her in his arms and kiss the colour back to her cheeks and the light back to her eyes! She was ill . . . because of him. Missing him. And what hell it had been for *him* these last few weeks! But he couldn't tell her, he couldn't say a word, or he would undo all the good that he had done so far.

He said: 'Just as you like, Dinah.'

Then he turned and strode on down the deck. And Dinah went blindly in the opposite direction, feeling the salt wind against her face, wondering how she would have the strength to go through with the next twelve days.

Pat didn't look well. He didn't look happy. Well, how could he be happy having hurt her so? And why was he going to Malta? Perhaps he was taking a long holiday. Perhaps there was some girl out in Malta whom he was going to see.

She saw him again that evening when she and her mother sat in the smoking-room, drinking sherry before dinner. Pat was on a stool at the bar. This time there was a woman with him. A woman older than Dinah, with reddish hair and an extremely good figure. She and Pat were drinking cocktails and laughing a lot. Every time Dinah heard Pat's laugh it shook her. That marvellously gay laugh of his. It really was not fair to put her to this strain. And who was the woman with the red hair? Perhaps *she* was the cause of all the trouble. How could Pat sit there laughing. Yet why not? *His* heart was not breaking. It was he who had ended their engagement.

Dinah went quickly out of the smoking-room, so that she could no longer hear his laughter. And she avoided going into the dining-saloon and went early to bed. Her mother was so anxious about her that Dinah did not let her see what she was feeling. She pretended to be sea-sick. But it was pure heart-sickness that sent Dinah to her bed that night, and drenched her pillow with tears long after Mrs Willis was asleep.

And while Dinah was crying herself to sleep, Pat Delaney was walking up and down the darkened deck in the cool night wind, talking to the red-haired woman whom he had only met a few hours ago, and who seemed interested in him. He was interested in her only as a sympathetic listener.

'Something's biting you badly,' the woman said to him, slipping an arm through his. She was attracted by the handsome boy who had such a tragic look in his Irish eyes.

He answered: 'It's much worse than that. I'm desperate. The girl I love and whom I once hoped to marry is on this boat and I hardly know what to do about it.'

'Doesn't she love you?'

'Yes.'

'Then what's the trouble?'

'I broke our engagement three weeks ago.'

'But, you lunatic, why?'

He told her and she listened and raised her brows. At the end she said: 'I think you've made a mistake. Your psychology is wrong. I think if you told her what you've told me she'd still want to marry you.'

'I think so, too,' said Pat, 'and that's exactly why I can't tell her.'

'You're quixotic — an idealist — and it doesn't pay.'

'Maybe not,' said Pat with a short laugh, 'but one has to be true to one's own nature and I've done what I consider to be the right thing.'

'Is it right to break that girl's heart?'

'Hearts don't break,' said Pat.

The red-headed woman said: 'That's where you're wrong. Somebody broke mine ten years ago and now I don't much care whether I live or die. I'm just drifting, my dear. You'd hate that nice girl of yours to drift, wouldn't you?'

'She'll never do that.'

'Don't be a fool. Tell her the truth.'

Pat said desperately: 'I can't. I won't. It wouldn't be fair.'

3

For the next forty-eight hours Dinah and Pat studiously avoided each other. Dinah caught glimpses of him and he of her, on the deck or in the saloons. Dinah's heartache went on remorselessly. But she put up a good show — mainly because of that woman with the red hair who was so constantly at Pat's side, and who, Dinah was confident, was the cause of her broken engagement.

On the third day out there was a cinema show on board. Mrs Willis was resting and Dinah came alone to see the film. Midway through, a man slipped into the empty chair beside her. She was electrified to find that it was Pat. He had not noticed her in the darkness, but the moment her face and form became familiar he said:

'Sorry! I didn't see you. Shall I find another place?'

'Don't bother,' she said coldly.

The film went on. They both stared at it without seeing a thing. Dinah's pulses were leaping. She had sat next to him so often in London cinemas. Always with her fingers curled in his, her body pressing against his side. Both of them experiencing the thrill of contact, Pat turning now and again to drop a kiss upon her hair, and whisper: '*Darlingest!*'

It was awful to think how everything had changed. Damn that red-headed woman, thought Dinah. Oh *damn* her.

When the picture was over and the lights flashed on, Dinah and Pat looked at each other for a moment, a tense unhappy look. Pat opened his lips as though to say something, then shut them again. Dinah said:

'Rather a good film.'

'Most enjoyable,' he said.

Then they walked away from each other.

Dinah went down to her cabin and looked at a calendar and thought:

'Nine more days of this hell. Nine more days and nights to Malta. Why in heaven's name didn't we choose to go on another boat?'

Two days later they reached Gibraltar. The weather changed. The grey sea became a shining, greeny-blue and the sun streamed down, bringing passengers out in sun-bathing suits on to the upper deck. The swimming-pool was filled, and deck games began in earnest.

The first dance of the voyage was held that same evening. A warmish evening with stars and moonlight as the ship moved away from Gibraltar.

Mrs Willis retired to bed early. Dinah contemplated doing the same. She really could not bear the thought of dancing; of seeing Pat with that red-haired creature in his arms. On the other hand, she asked herself why she should make her life wretched because of him. He had betrayed their love, and he was not worth all this grief and sickness of soul. Why not put on one of her new lovely evening dresses and find some man to dance with her. It should be easy.

It was very easy. Dinah in a white evening dress, was quite the most entrancing figure on board. She had a circle of young men round her in a minute, all asking for dances. She laughed and flirted and hoped that Pat would see her, which he did. Pat in evening clothes, a carnation in his buttonhole, handsome and debonair, dancing quite a number of times with his red-haired friend, could hardly tear his gaze from that beloved figure in white. But when they passed each other in the dance, he avoided her gaze.

Everything seemed all right until the band started to play! 'Thanks for the Memory.'

Then Dinah disengaged herself from the arm of the boy who was dancing with her and said that she wanted to 'fetch a handkerchief'.

She rushed away to a part of the deck where it was dark and lonely. She stood there shaking, her face buried in her hands.

Oh, Pat, Pat, and they had only just reached Gibraltar. Would this acute misery ease up by the time they got to Malta? Or was there to be no respite?

Then she became conscious that she was no longer alone. Her hands fell from her face. She saw Pat standing there before her. Pat with a face that looked strained and white, and eyes as unhappy as her own. He said: 'Dinah! are you all right? I saw you run away. That was our tune . . . '

'How dare you,' she said passionately, miserably, 'how dare you follow me and say such things to me after what you have done.'

'It's too much for me, Dinah,' he said.

'Too much for *you*? What do you think it is for me?'

'I've never stopped thinking what it's been for you. The thought of that has upset me much more than any thought of myself.'

138

Dinah looked at him, wide-eyed, resentful. 'I don't understand you. Why should *you* be miserable? You broke our engagement, didn't you?'

'Yes. But I'm beginning to believe I did wrong.'

Dinah laughed wildly. 'You haven't changed your mind, have you? Has the red-headed woman turned you down this evening?'

Pat stared at her. 'What do you mean? What's the red-headed woman got to do with it?'

'Isn't she your new girlfriend?'

'No. Definitely no. I only met her four days ago. She's been kind. She's told me what a fool I am. That's all. Tonight I believe her. Dinah, I just can't go on . . . I've no strength left. The sight of you and the sound of our signature tune has flattened me completely.'

Dinah put a hand to her forehead in a bewildered way.

'Honestly, I don't understand you. If you feel like this, why did you break with me in the first place?'

He said irrelevantly: 'Tell me that you still love me, for lord's sake.'

Then Dinah burst into tears. 'You're a cad to ask it. You're a swine, when you know — '

She got no further than that. Pat caught her to him and soundlessly buried his face against her curls, then kissed her mouth. Kissed her, until her lips opened and responded feverishly to his . . . until they were clinging together in an embrace more desperately passionate than any they had ever shared. And when at length he lifted his head, Pat said: 'That was like heaven . . . heaven after the hell.'

'Oh darling,' said Dinah, 'if you feel like that, why, why . . . ?'

He told her then, blurted out the story helplessly, in the grip of the strongest emotion of all . . . his overwhelming love for this one girl in the world.

Three weeks ago, he said, his firm had crashed . . . Big people though they were, they had met with a colossal set-back and they had been forced to dismiss most of their staff, including himself. It had been a crushing blow when he had expected so soon to be married. In the circumstances, faced with no job and having no private income, it would have been impossible for him to marry Dinah. Particularly as her father was well off and she had been used to everything that she had wanted. He had battled with himself for many bitter hours, he told Dinah, and had decided in the long run it would be unfair of him to carry on with the engagement. Equally unfair to give her his reason for breaking it, since he knew she would immediately offer to marry him just the same. That would not have been possible and he did not feel it would be right to ask her to eke out a long engagement while he built up his future again.

'That's the whole story, darlingest,' said Pat with his arm round Dinah, holding her close, 'and now perhaps you'll understand what hell I've been through. It was sending my very life from me when I sent you that goodbye note.'

Dinah gave a long sigh. Her eyes were brighter than the stars in the heavens. Her face bore a rapt look. She whispered:

'Oh, how wonderful! How *wonderful* to think that's why you broke with me. You did it for my sake.'

'And now I've been weak and let it all out.'

She put her arms round his neck. 'Thank God for the weakness. Pat, Pat, it's been driving me mad to think you didn't love me, didn't want me any more. I don't think I could have borne it much longer.'

'My sweet,' he said, and kissed her again feverishly.

Then Dinah said:

'But what are you doing on this boat? Why are you going to Malta?'

'To a firm of engineers. I was lucky in a way. One of the heads of the firm who held me rather in respect knew of something going out there. Nothing much of a salary. But a start, anyhow. So I took it and booked my passage, never dreaming you'd be on the same boat.'

'What sort of a salary?' asked Dinah.

'Half what I was getting before.'

Dinah made a rapid calculation. 'With my allowance we could still do it,' she said excitedly.

He protested. 'Darling, I can't possibly ask you — '

'I'm asking *you*,' she broke in, 'in fact I'm telling you, Pat, that I can't go on without you and that if you refuse to marry me, even on your small salary, I shall just curl up and die. You couldn't allow me to die, could you, Pat?'

'I should want to die with you, if you did,' he said.

'Then,' said Dinah, 'we'll go down to Mother and tell her everything, and I shall get off at Malta. I shall marry you there, and Mummy will have to make the rest of the voyage alone. Yes, Pat,

143

you shan't be allowed to escape me again. There might be lots of red-headed women in Malta.'

'I don't particularly like red-headed women. Oh, darling! . . . '

Dinah surrendered herself to another feverish embrace. Then, with a long-drawn sigh, she quoted:

'*You may have been a headache, but you never were a bore. How lovely it was.*'

Pat said: 'I've got to take you, Dinah, whether it's right or wrong. I see I've got to take you.'

'I've brought my ring with me,' said Dinah. 'Let's go and find it and put it back where it belongs.'

Three Kisses

1

If there was one thing that Victoria Katherine Porter could not withstand, it was a direct, if unspoken, challenge from a confirmed woman-hater.

That was her signal for a big attack, and she nearly always won. She looked small and defenceless, but her weapons were deadly. She was lovely. She had personality — and courage. Nobody who knew Vicky ever dared her do anything.

The daughter of a General in the Indian Army, she had spent a good deal of her early life in India, and on one occasion when a stupid boy, who did not know Vicky so well, dared her to dive into a crocodile-infested river, she had jumped straight in and everybody had had heart-failure except Vicky, who oughtn't to have come out alive. But she did — laughing. Which was the way that she came out of most of her big love-affairs. But then it was generally Vicky who dealt the death-blow to the romance. She had never found anyone who could tame her.

Her mother maintained that it was because she had not stuck to the solemn and practical name which she had been given. As Victoria she might, the harassed and ever-anxious Mrs Porter maintained, have emulated the example of the great queen. But as Vicky — she was an irresponsible will-o'-the-wisp, and it was woe to the man who chased the flickering light in her golden, black-lashed eyes, and who lost himself in the enchantment of her smile.

It was Vicky's twenty-first birthday just before Christmas. Her mother made her accept Harriet Farnway's invitation to her Christmas house-party up in Scotland.

Lady Farnway lived in one of the loveliest estates on the border. She was the mother of a family of three children, and although young and gay, the sort of wife and mother that Mrs Porter always hoped Vicky would make in time. Mrs Porter thought it would be good for Vicky to have a family Christmas away from her mother. Vicky was always at her worst when she was present, as though that gentle and worried lady inspired her to mischief. So Mrs Porter betook herself and the gouty General to a Spa for health's sake, and Vicky caught the night train to Scotland.

She could have had a sleeper had she wanted one. But she didn't. She loathed sleepers. She preferred to sit upright in a comfortable first-class carriage and smoke and read until she dozed. It was thus that she found herself — by quite a strange coincidence — alone with a remarkably good-looking young man who appeared also to dislike sleepers and was prepared for a more spartan journey North.

The train moved out of the light and shelter of King's Cross into the bitter cold of the December night, and a hint of fog. But the famous express cut contemptuously through the yellow vapours and gathered speed.

Vicky, huddled in tweeds and furs, removed a feathered cap from her chestnut curls and cast a look at the young man who sat opposite.

'Nice,' she thought. Masculine, tweed coat and grey flannels. The old school tie. Shining brogues. Six-foot-two of tanned, virile British manhood with the bluest eyes Vicky had ever seen. She hoped they would glance often in her direction. They did, but without the slightest sign of interest. The casual and uninterested look was the first shot which made Vicky sit up and consider the fact that there was going to be war! And the next thing was a peep at the label on the luggage. In a flash it was revealed to her that this was Mr Nicholas Carden, and that he, too, was bound for Doonkirk. He was the Nicholas of whom Harriet Farnway had often spoken to Vicky. Nicholas the misogynist — who had been at school with Harriet's husband, and had withstood all her match-making efforts.

On one of those long-distance calls which only cost less after six-thirty, Vicky and Harriet had discussed this very Nicholas.

'There's a job for you, Vicky,' Harriet had said. 'I've asked Nicky to the house-party especially to meet you. He's an angel but so shy. Thinks all women are out to marry him — which of course they are. He's got a marvellous job — travels for a big oil company, and has no relations.'

To which Vicky had replied: 'Darling, how divine! We *ought* to have fun. 'Vicky and Nicky'. I'll make a rhyme about it.'

And she made lots of rhymes, none of which she showed to Mrs Porter. And here she was sharing a carriage alone with Nicky on an all-night journey to Scotland. Could anything have been more effectively staged?

Vicky lost no time in introducing herself.

'I simply *must* speak,' she said, leaning forward and smiling at the young man who had settled himself down with an evening paper. 'I'm sure you're Nicholas Carden. I'm Victoria Porter, and we're both going up to Harriet Farnway's Christmas party.'

The young man lowered the paper, reddened with embarrassment, cleared his throat, then acknowledged the fact that he was Nicholas Carden, and that he was going up to Harriet's party, added that it was a filthy night, and returned to his paper.

'Gosh!' said Vicky to herself, and considered which of her weapons she would have to use. Certainly it was going to be a divine journey.

Behind the paper, Nicholas Carden glowered. Victoria Porter, eh? He'd heard of her. Who hadn't? If her name wasn't in the paper reporting the fact that she had been fined for exceeding the speed limit, her photograph was in all the expensive journals or some paper announcing an engagement, only made to be broken. He had no use for that sort of girl. Just a little Society 'tough'. Damned pretty. He had to admit that. Pretty voice, too. He liked soft voices in women. (If he liked anything about them!) But he didn't, often. He was a bachelor, and a bachelor he intended to remain. Harriet had married one of his best friends, so he accepted Harriet and took no notice of her efforts to attach him to one young female or another of her choosing. It was the Farnway kids he adored. Especially young Nicholas, aged four, who was his godson. He was going up to Doonkirk for the express purpose of spending Christmas with the kids. He supposed he'd have to put up with the adults.

A beguiling voice murmured: 'Could you lift my suitcase down for me just a moment?'

At once he abandoned his paper, stood up and lifted down the covered dressing-case, which bore the initials V.K.P., and handed it to Victoria Porter. He hoped that would be all, but found himself unlocking the case for her, caught a glimpse of something disturbing in peachy silk, peeping from a fold of tissue paper, also a delicate aroma of gardenia perfume and retreated fearfully back to his corner.

But that was only the beginning. There were lots of things Vicky wanted. A cigarette. A match for it. And he had to have one, too, and smoke it with her. And they had to talk, all about the Farnways, and what a darling Harriet was, and Harriet's husband Jack. Hadn't *he* been at school with Jack? She *must* hear all about it. And there were lots of other things she wanted to know. A surprising number of things that she knew about, too. His job, and his much-travelled life, and this, and that, and the other.

Never had Nicholas Carden been drawn into so much conversation about nothing in particular. Yet it wasn't so boring. Vicky was a vivacious conversationalist, and he had to admit that she was also intelligent, though rumour had it that she behaved like a little idiot from time to time.

He wondered how old she was. She looked about sixteen, sitting there with the fur coat open just enough to show a slender figure in a well-cut tweed skirt and pale blue woolly jumper, and a wide gold choker round a long, slender throat. Nails too red and lips too red. And yet she had a fresh look. Marvellous skin. It was the first time in Nicholas' life that he had ever taken so much notice of a woman from the physical point of view. He became rather ashamed of it, and abandoned conversation.

But Vicky wasn't going to let things rest at that. She liked this young man. The fact that he was shy amused her. She could sense that he was frightened of her. That, in itself, was intriguing. If anyone was going to make him come out of his shell, she would, if only to boast to Harriet. Men were awfully stupid, Vicky decided. Even the hardest bitten of them could be gulled in the long run. She wondered if she would ever find anyone whom she really wanted to marry. He would have to be a super-man.

She hinted that she was thirsty. Nicholas saw that it was no use trying to read his paper, and folded it up. He rang for a drink for Vicky. Coffee. She wouldn't have alcohol, oh no! She never touched it, she told him. He was edified by that. He thought that the only remorse that girls like Victoria Porter ever experienced was alcoholic!

He himself was a moderate drinker. He found himself ordering a double gin tonight. Two, three and four hours elapsed. The express was out of the fog area and running frantically North-wards.

Vicky talked again. About herself this time.

'You know the world. You've travelled a lot, and I'm sure you see things as they really are,' she said to Nicholas, with a wistful little-girl look in her lovely eyes. 'I wish you'd tell me what to do with my life. I'm so sick of it all

— the futility of things. You're a person who does *real* things. If only I could, too . . .'

'I'm sure you could,' he said awkwardly, and was flattered and a little touched because she wished to unburden her soul to him. After another half-hour he was inclined to believe that Victoria Porter was much maligned by the Press and by rumour. She was really a very nice child — just needed guidance. There was nothing tough about her. Perhaps nobody understood her. He could sympathize. Nobody had ever understood him, until tonight. But this young girl had an extraordinary comprehension.

'You're concerned with the big things of life — a real man's life — you don't want the artificiality of Society and the chains of matrimony. You're so wise,' she had said just now.

He found himself wanting to tell her more about himself. At two in the morning he was sure that he knew everything about *her*. She was lonely.

157

And neither of her two engagements had been a success because, well, the men just hadn't understood. Poor little thing!

At 4 a.m. Vicky, instead of being tired, was wide awake, very elated, and storing up heaps of funny things that she was going to tell Harriet about this young man who was just as easily hoodwinked as the rest of them. At the same time she thought: 'He's frightfully nice. I really rather like him.'

In the early hours of the morning it grew cold. There was a draught blowing in from the corridor. Vicky shivered. Nicholas saw the shiver and hastened to find her rug and wrap it around her. She lay tucked up on the seat opposite him, looking so young that he thought all kinds of tender things connected with Christmas, with kids, stockings being hung up, and mistletoe.

Perhaps Vicky sensed that thought of his about mistletoe, and turned hers to kisses. She wondered if Nicholas Carden had ever kissed a woman in his life! Anyhow it was time he learned. She gave him a sweet and drowsy smile through veiled lashes.

'Good night, Nicky. May I call you that? Harriet always does, and it goes with my name. They call me — Vicky.'

'I like Victoria best,' he said.

'Do you?'

The train swayed a little and he swayed in her direction. He did like her — quite a lot, and his senses suddenly swam as she had intended they should, straight into the lure of those sleepy eyes and red appealing mouth.

It was, as Vicky afterwards described to Harriet, most fitting that just as they crossed the border, Nicholas should cross his particular boundary line. He bent forward and kissed her. And once having tasted the nectar of Vicky's lips, Nicholas Carden learned to like women a little better.

'Merry Christmas,' was what he said, clearing his throat, red to the roots of his hair as he moved away from Vicky, and realized that was an absurd remark because there were still two days to go to Christmas. But he felt he had to apologize for losing his head.

Vicky, who had enjoyed her victory, gave him a starry smile and whispered: 'I'm sure we'll be marvellous friends.' She told herself that that would be the first of many kisses before they reached their destination. But to her surprise it was the last. Nicholas settled in his corner and seemed furiously embarrassed and shame-faced. He hardly spoke another word to Vicky during the rest of the journey.

2

Once installed in Doonkirk Hall, Vicky and Nicholas were more or less swallowed up in the crowd. And it *was* a crowd! Harriet liked her particular cronies about her and Jack had a big shooting party.

It was all a lot of fun. Doonkirk wore a festive air. The great hall with its rich panelling, centuries old, decorated with stags' heads, and the gleaming crossed swords of fighting ancestors, was gaily hung with holly and mistletoe and well warmed by an enormous log fire.

The best hour at Doonkirk was five o'clock tea when the men had come in from shooting, glad to relax in the warmth, eat a big tea and receive congratulations on the day's sport from the fairer members of the party. When the three Farnway children came down from the nursery, everybody played games, caught up in the Christmas spirit, until the old Scottish nanny swept her bairns upstairs again. With the advent of cocktails, a more subtle and adult atmosphere prevailed.

On the first day of her arrival, it was at this hour that Vicky confided to one girl and another what she had already poured into her friend Harriet's ears — the story of the journey from London, with Nicholas, and how she had conquered his famous bashfulness. Which news was lapped up by the more kittenish of the assembly as though it were rich cream. *Nicholas Carden had kissed Vicky Porter!* A victory indeed. But then Vicky was unique. The most glamorous of her sex. And what was the next move? Would he kiss her again? Vicky said, 'Yes.' Undoubtedly. And not because of any mistletoe. Tomorrow was Christmas Eve, the time for general rejoicing, and she had every intention that the sun-bronzed giant, with the blue eyes and idealistic mouth, should rejoice in Vicky's particular fashion.

Harriet went from one to another of her guests, the perfect hostess, secretly planning who should sit beside who at her table, and what might result from pairing off A with B. When it came to Vicky, she said:

'It would be too divine if you could really wake Nicky up, even for a little affair! We must all help — not that I think you need any! Jack says it's time Nicky got married.'

'I don't think I want to get married,' said Vicky.

And she didn't, in spite of the fact that her mother was so anxious she should settle down, like Harriet, and have a lovely home and three lovely children.

Looking through the crowd, Vicky watched Nicholas Carden hoist his godson on his shoulders. He was rather like a Viking, she thought; much taller and more splendid than any of the other men who sat before the fire, saying: 'That was a pretty shot of yours! . . . ' or, 'Very sporting effort

— those partridges were flying damned high . . . '

Nicholas was more concerned with the children than with shooting stories. He adored kids. And Vicky, her lovely eyes serious and thoughtful, decided that Nicholas would make a very good father. He had seemed shy and awkward in her presence today — she supposed it was because he had kissed her in the train. But now and then she became aware of the fact that he had seated himself beside her, or was smiling shyly at her. She guessed he was intrigued, despite himself. She knew, too, that he was very much too nice to be played with. But it was Christmas, and she *did* want to play, just a tiny, *weeny* bit.

Nicholas was lifting Harriet's six-year-old girl up in his arms now. Vicky heard him say:

'Who's going to fill *your* stocking tomorrow night, young woman!'

'Father Christmas!' was the reply, followed by a scream of delight as the young woman was hoisted on to the shoulder which her brother had just vacated.

Vicky, a cigarette in a long black holder between her red lips, strolled up to the little group and looked through her lashes at Nicholas.

'Do you think if *I* hung up *my* stocking, Father Christmas would be kind to me?'

He looked down at her. She saw the deep red creep up quickly beneath his tan. His eyes crinkled at the corners.

'Only if you're good,' he said gravely. 'You've got to be frightfully *good*, you know, if you want a visit from Father Christmas — so I'm told.'

She gave a little liquid laugh. It set his heart shaking. She was only a child, he told himself, and the most adorable of them all. He hadn't forgiven himself for kissing her in the train, and yet he wanted so much to kiss her again. He had never felt like that about any other woman.

'I'm *terribly* good,' she murmured,

165

'so I shall hang up my stocking and pray.'

Which made Nicholas worry frantically in his mind as to what he could find to put in that stocking, which was a gossamer nylon sheath to the loveliest and slenderest of legs.

They danced that night at Doonkirk. Most of Vicky's dances were with Nicholas. Her tawny curls barely touched his shoulder. She was virginal and exquisite in a white filmy dress with white gardenias in her hair. She danced like a dream. Nicholas trod twice clumsily on a little sandalled foot, apologized, held his partner more closely, and wondered why anybody had ever said anything about Vicky Porter except that she was an angel from heaven.

Harriet Farnway watched from the doorway, delighted, then sent a discreet message to the man who was working the big radio gramophone. There issued the seductive strains of: 'The touch of your lips.'

166

Nicholas' blue eyes burned and blurred a little, and Vicky gave a shy, answering smile and her lashes drooped. His fingers tightened over hers until she winced. She had the most curious sensation in her throat as though she wanted to cry. Not at all like Vicky. Simultaneously there flashed through her mind a feeling of remorse because she used all her youth and loveliness and charm to ensnare the hearts of men and never allowed herself to be snared. And she was sorry that she had told anybody at Doonkirk about that kiss in the train.

3

On Christmas Eve there were more parties. Shooting, dancing, a whole lot of fun. Vicky was the gayest of the gay, pursued by all the young men in Harriet's party. Without much success, because there was always six-foot-two of Nicholas Carden hovering around her. And it was whispered at Doonkirk that Nicky Carden was vulnerable after all. And they called Vicky 'little Miss Victorious', whilst bets were made by the catty as to what Vicky would do with her prey and how long he would last.

But Nicholas Carden saw Vicky only as a misunderstood angel — a child, mischievous at heart, without real guile. He felt terribly protective and tender towards her. During dinner, seated on her left, he pulled crackers with her, put a foolish cap on his head and thought life intoxicating. He said: 'Are you going to hang up that stocking tonight?'

'Um,' said Vicky, removing a cone of pink tissue and gold paper from her curly head.

He was caught by a note of depression in her voice.

'Is anything wrong?' he asked.

'No,' she said. 'Except that you told me and the kids that one has to be awfully good to have one's stocking filled by Father Christmas.'

'Then why worry?' he said.

She turned from him and swallowed a drink hastily. The man on the other side of her, Major Hallum, whispered: 'I say, Vicky, you're fairly mopping up old Carden. Little devil, aren't you?'

He was exceedingly astonished when Vicky turned a pair of furious eyes upon him and whispered back through her teeth: 'Shut up, Tommy, and don't be a bore.'

Later that night, Harriet Farnway approached Nicholas and asked him if he would be an angel, dress up as

Father Christmas and fill the children's stockings.

'I've got all the doings, beard and wig and so on,' she said, 'and you know what the babes are. They might wake up. And if they open an eye and see a figure that *isn't* Papa Noel, they'll be *so* disillusioned. You'd be too divine doing it for me, darling.'

Nicholas said that he would love to do it for her, and his thoughts immediately flashed to a gossamer stocking which he would dearly like to fill. But, of course, that couldn't be. He'd give *her* a present in the morning. He had motored twenty miles to the nearest town this morning to buy her something. And in a town that seemed to sell nothing but haggis and short-bread, he had been driven almost insane. Finally he had found a book of classic poems. He hoped she would like them. The leather binding was good, anyhow.

Harriet had things all worked out. The Christmas Eve party didn't break up until midnight, and then she hustled all her guests off to bed, and said they mustn't be too late, because everybody had to get up and come down to breakfast with the children and open their parcels. There'd been a good deal of work under the mistletoe, in which Vicky had had most of the make-up removed from her face, but not by Nicholas. And neither had she let Nicholas see any of the other men kissing her. But each time she had been caught and kissed she had felt furious and put a lot more lipstick on her mouth in an irritable way.

The more people chaffed her about Nicky Carden, the more she resented it. She tried to tell herself that it wouldn't do to become serious and that she must 'snap out of it'.

But Harriet had plans. The spirit of mischief was bubbling in the young mother of three, and when Nicholas had been decked out in the scarlet robes, white wig and beard of Father Christmas, and given a sack of toys to carry over his shoulder, she crept with him down the wide, dimly lit corridor. Nobody was supposed to see. But plenty did see, peeping through their doors, because they had been let into the joke.

Nicholas, unsuspecting, stole into a room which was pointed out to him. He didn't know the geography of the house too well. His own room was in another wing, and if Harriet said that the kids were in this room, then they were.

'Don't turn on the lights, for heaven's sake,' she whispered. 'And just lay the things at the bottom of the bed.'

So Nicholas entered the room and stood a moment in the darkness, hoping he wouldn't knock anything over, or make a noise. Then he became conscious of two strange sensations. A wind with the icy breath of snow in it blowing in from an open window — and a perfume of gardenias. *Vicky's familiar perfume.* His nose wrinkled. He was baffled. Surely in here there should be an odour of talcum — *not* the subtle scent which he had grown to associate with Vicky's presence.

He lifted the sack from his shoulders, laid it gingerly down, picked out a parcel, and, groping like a blind man, advanced to what he thought was one of the youngsters' beds. Now, where were the stockings? There wasn't a bed-rail. This was a big divan. Where the devil was he? And then . . .

A movement in the bed. A soft voice whispering:

'Who's there?'

Nicholas stood aghast. Rooted to the spot he stood. Before he could speak, a light had been switched on and revealed to him Vicky Porter sitting up in the bed, looking like a beautiful little girl with flushed cheeks and tumbled curls. But she was not wearing a very 'little girl' nightgown, for it was of black chiffon, and through it gleamed the whitest of white skins. Nicholas went all dazed and stupid, and could not get a word out. Vicky stared at the apparition in the red gown and white beard. Then she burst into laughter.

With both hands cupping her cheeks she said: 'Why, it's Father Christmas! Then I must have been a good girl after all. How *marvellous*!'

Dumbfounded, Nicholas stared, trying to work out in his confused mind whether he had just made a mistake and come into the wrong room, or whether Harriet had gone mad and forgotten where her children slept, or if the whole thing was a put-up job. Anyhow, he picked up the bag and turned to fly.

'Dreadfully sorry — most ghastly mistake,' he stammered.

'But it isn't!' said Vicky. 'You can't go away. Please, Father Christmas, haven't you got a present for me? Oh, please . . .'

He stood irresolute. A small hand caught his.

'Please!' echoed the beguiling voice.

Then Nicholas for the second time in his life lost his head. He just dropped the bag, pulled off his white beard, went down on one knee, took that charming, beseeching face between his hands and kissed the red lips long and ardently.

Vicky went all limp, and responded to that kiss with her soul in it.

But rapture was short-lived. The silence of the night was broken by a scream of laughter outside the door and a jumble of voices. Nicholas struggled to his feet, conscious of a great many people circling round him. Harriet, in a paroxysm of mirth, Jack Farnway, looking a bit sheepish, Tommy Hallum, in pyjamas and dressing-gown, with a monocle in his eye, wagging a finger of protest, Vera Princep, who was one of the biggest scandal-mongers in the world, creaming her face, as she ran in, to see the fun. They were all screaming together.

'Too divine . . . Father Christmas filling Vicky's stocking . . . '

'Who *is* Father Christmas?'

'It's Nicky Carden. And there's no mistletoe in here, naughty boy!'

'What have you chosen for her, old boy? A woolly lamb, or teddy bear?'

And so on, till a final remark made Nicky's ears burn, and his blood boil.

'That was *beautifully* staged, Vicky.'

Beautifully staged! So it *was* a put-up job. And they were all in the joke, these cackling women, these men — damned silly fellows, who were making wise-cracks about Father Christmas 'stepping a bit out of character'. And Vicky was in it, too. Vicky had staged it. That was the thought which stung Nicholas. She wasn't the angel he'd thought her, but just a heartless flirt who liked to make her conquests public. The Victoria Porter who was the idol of Society. It was the last time he'd make a fool of himself over any woman. The first and the last.

Harriet caught his arm and said: 'It was only a joke, Nicky. Don't look so grim.'

He pulled off the wig, threw the sack of toys at her feet, and said: 'I'm glad your little jest was so much appreciated. Would you mind getting someone else to take my place. I'm a bit clumsy for the job.'

He marched away, and Jack Farnway nodded at his wife.

'Now you've upset old Nicky. You know he can't bear to be in the limelight. It was a damn silly joke, anyhow.'

'It wasn't. It was a very good one,' said Harriet indignantly.

But when she went back into Vicky's bedroom, she wasn't so sure about that. For Vicky was lying with her face buried in the pillow, crying as though her heart would break. Vicky in tears! A sight that Harriet had never seen before, and which revealed quite a new side to Vicky's character.

'It was a damn silly joke!' Vicky wept bitterly. 'And he thinks I was in it and that I ridiculed him in front of everybody. I wish it had *never* happened.'

'Why, darling,' said Harriet, 'I'd no idea — '

'Oh, go away and leave me alone!' interrupted Vicky.

'I'll explain to Nicky that you weren't in it.'

But Vicky turned a hot, tear-stained face to her and stammered:

'You won't do anything of the sort . . . I know what he thinks of me, and it'll be no use explaining. That could only make things worse. If there's to be any apology, I'll make it myself.'

'Oh dear,' said Vicky's hostess, genuinely sorry that her plans had so miscarried, 'and it's Christmas Eve, too.'

'I don't care if it's Michaelmas! said Vicky, and burst into tears again.

But there were no tears anywhere else at Doonkirk. The guests were all heartily amused by the visit which 'Father Christmas' had paid the famous Vicky Porter. The whole house seethed with quips and jests, that next morning when everybody gathered for breakfast in the big dining-room to exchange the compliments of the season.

But two people were missing from that table. They were the subjects of the jest. And nowhere could they be found. Lady Farnway was informed by the valet that Mr Carden had risen very early. He had met him down in the hall, and Mr Carden had said that he was going for a walk through the snow. But that was at seven, and now it was nine, and he hadn't come back. It was snowing hard, too. Doonkirk awoke to a white world. The fir-trees were powdered with feathery flakes. There was a foot of snow on the ground. Not much weather for a walk.

Harriet felt rather anxious.

Had anyone seen anything of Vicky?

Yes. Somebody had heard from somebody else that she had borrowed Jack's small car and taken it down the road.

'A car out in this snow!' exclaimed Harriet. 'The girl's mad!'

But Vicky had set out in that car not in any way mad, but in a fever-heat of worry over Nicky. He had gone out at seven and hadn't come back. What had happened to him? It was snowing so hard that she could scarcely see a yard ahead. The windscreen-wipers could not cope with the heavy white flakes, and the moisture froze on the glass as it formed. The wheels slithered over the snow in the brownish tracks that had been made by a milk-van that morning. It was one of the severe blizzards that they had occasionally up in Doonkirk, and this was a particularly lonely part of the country. Of course Nicholas knew it, Vicky told herself. But he might have left the beaten track, slipped and broken a leg. A dozen and one fears assailed her. And with those fears came the rushing knowledge that she loved Nicholas Carden. Loved him as she had never loved any man in her life. She felt nothing but an abandonment of grief and regret because she had set out to be his undoing; had laughed at him and boasted of her conquest. Now it had all come back on her and she, herself, was conquered. And he despised her. She knew that he did. When he had walked out of her room last night, he had given her one awful look, withering her. He believed that she had staged that scene in her bedroom on purpose. That she had kissed him lightly, that the kisses were all part of the joke. Oh, but they weren't! The one in the train hadn't meant much. But last night — that had meant a whole lot. Everything, in fact.

Nicholas was shy and sensitive. Perhaps he was so badly upset by last night that he just felt he didn't care what happened to him. Perhaps that was why he had taken this suicidal walk in the snowstorm.

Vicky drove Farnway's car down the road, straining her eyes to see through the twirling flakes, peering to the right and the left, as though she fully expected to discover Nicky's body in the ditch, at any moment.

And this was Christmas morning! A morning when bells would soon be ringing joyous messages, and everybody should be happy and at peace, and bear each other goodwill. Vicky felt choked. Every time the tyres slipped and skidded — it made her heart jolt. But she managed to right the skid and drive on. She *must* find Nicky. And if he wasn't in this direction, she must turn and try the other.

She drove for the next hour, this way and that, down roads and lanes, slipping and racing the engine as the wheels slurred over the ground, half blinded by the continual effort to see through the snow-caked wind-screen; perished with cold, hungry, and ready to cry.

And she did not find Nicholas. At length, defeated and dejected, Vicky managed to get the car back to Doonkirk Hall, by which time she was exhausted, and her hands so frozen that she could scarcely grip the steering wheel.

When she stepped out of the car and walked into the house she staggered a little, and had a horrible feeling she was going to faint. She managed to get to the door of the dining-room and opening it, saw the man for whom she had been searching under such gruelling conditions. No suicide, no corpse in the ditch, no bitter and disillusioned man stumbling through a blizzard. But a quite sane and apparently cheerful Nicholas eating a big breakfast with the Farnway children on either side of him, unwrapping parcels, uttering whoops of joy.

Vicky gave Nicholas a bitter look. So that was all he cared! What a little fool she'd been. Last night hadn't meant anything like so much to him as it had meant to her. The joke was certainly on her this time. Harriet came rushing forward.

'Vicky! You poor lamb. You look all in. Where *have* you been?'

Vicky gave a feeble smile. Her lips were blue under the rouge. The room went black about her. She heard herself say as from a distance:

'I went to look for . . . Father Christmas . . . You see, I've been bad . . . so he didn't fill . . . stocking . . . '

And after that, no more.

She came back to consciousness to find herself lying on the sofa in the

183

library. Somebody was moistening her lips with brandy, and patting her hands. A deep, anxious voice kept on repeating her name.

'Vicky, Vicky! Oh, my dear, open your eyes, *please*!'

She did as she was told and looked straight up into the brown face of Nicky Carden. Nicky on his knees beside her — just as he had been last night. And his eyes were looking just as blurred and ardent, so Vicky gave a great sob of thankfulness and held out both her arms.

'Oh, Nicky — Nicky!'

He took her into a warm, close embrace.

'You went out to look for me. Through that snow. You were half frozen — half dead — you poor little thing. I shall never forget how you looked. Why did you do it? Why did you bother about me? What did it matter to you what happened to me?'

She clung to him and whispered: 'It mattered terribly. I didn't mean to make fun of you last night. You thought I did and you were furious with me. You must have thought me a little beast, and I — '

'I did until Harriet explained that you weren't in it,' he interrupted.

Then Vicky felt a sudden need for honesty.

'I *was* in it up to a point. I wasn't serious in the train. And I laughed behind your back when I first got to Doonkirk. But I regretted it. Now I regret everything — my other engagements — the way I've fooled through life. It's different loving you — so very different, Nicky, I swear it!'

'Do you mean that, sweet?'

'Don't you believe me?' she counter-questioned.

He looked down into her swimming eyes. He covered both her cold hands with kisses and said:

'Yes. I do. And I want to marry you, Victoria Porter. And you're never going to be allowed to fool around with anyone again — except me.'

Then for the third time he kissed her and whispered: 'Merry Christmas . . . ' But this time he added: ' . . . My *darling*!'

Lady Farnway, bearing a cup of coffee, looked through the library door, looked twice, and then with all her match-making instincts entirely satisfied, took the cup of coffee out again, and softly closed the door.

Instinct

It was out in Malaga in the early spring of this year, when I was sitting in the Spanish Club drinking iced coffee, that I first saw the Langdens and heard their story.

The retired doctor who was one of our party, and who for health's sake spent most of the year in this Southern watering place with its perfect climate, called my attention to the little party, or I might not have noticed them. I was so busy looking through the plate-glass windows at the streets which had just been washed by a watering-cart and were glittering and steaming in the hot sunlight; at the passing tourists, the Spanish women mostly in black, the men with their sombreros, their lazy graceful gait and the swarms of dirty children who pressed wizened faces against the glass, whining for a *peseta*.

Spain held glamour for me. Not so much this busy port, but the country beyond with its white walls and arches, its blue skies and even bluer sea, and the hyacinth shadow of sombre mountains fringing the road that leads to Gibraltar.

But my doctor friend found something even more glamorous to attract my attention. A woman who came into the Spanish Club followed by her husband and two children. When I say children, the girl might have been about fourteen, and the boy a year or two younger.

'You're a writer,' said the doctor. 'There's an interesting lot for you. A history behind them that would be copy for any author. Take a look at them. Tell me what you see.'

I did so. I saw first and foremost the woman, in her thirties, obviously English, well-bred, soignée, hair bleached almost to silver by the sun, and in contrast a tanned skin which was very attractive. She was as slender as the

190

young girl beside her.

As she sat down on one of the long plush seats and laid a couple of parcels on the marble-topped table, she smiled up at the man. I thought her smile a frank and lovely thing. My attention turned to him. Also fair and smart and typically English; and even in the dim light of the Club I could discern the fact that he had very blue eyes. But he was lined — looked older than his wife. His hair was grey.

He lit a cigarette for her and, as he gave it to her, touched her cheek and whispered something in a way which might have suggested that he was her lover. But my friend, the doctor, was telling me they had been married for seventeen years.

'They're a good-looking couple,' I said, 'but there's an air of tragedy about him. What is it?'

'That's what I'm going to tell you,' he said. 'But look at the children first of all. What do you notice about them?'

I thought the girl resembled neither

of her parents, except that her eyes were blue, which contrasted strangely with her olive face and black hair. Hers was the ripe dark beauty of Spain. The boy on the other hand was slim and fair like his mother.

I urged my doctor friend for the story. And when I had heard it I was profoundly intrigued. I'll let you have the whole thing as I picture it, and in my own language. I have often thought about the little foursome, although I never saw them again after that day in Malaga. My doctor gave away no names so I shall use those that I create for them.

Peta Langden, eighteen years ago, was interested in nothing much but breeding Irish wolf-hounds. She had married Richard Langden because she was in love with him in her way, but she was, if anything, under-sexed and physically she looked like a boy, and was more often to be seen in a shirt and riding-breeches than frilly clothes. She spent most of her time in the kennels and was absorbed in the care of the big hounds. Some said she moved her slender limbs with the same swift grace of the animals. Anyhow she knew her job, and her kennel name was fast becoming known in the dog world.

Richard Langden had been in the Navy in his youth. When he married Peta he had finished with the sea and was settled at the Admiralty in a good job which he deserved, for he had both brains and integrity of character.

He fell in love with Peta the first time he saw her, at a dog show, standing straight and slim with a great wolf-hound on a leash on either side of her. He had spoken to one of the dogs, then to her. She had answered in the frank, unaffected way which had won his heart almost as much as her fragile beauty. She was vastly intriguing. She looked, he told her, much too ethereal to run dog kennels. Yet she knew how to manage those big brutes. In fact she had an almost magnetic influence over the most difficult of them.

At a later day, when she showed him a new litter of puppies and picked up one of the little things and snuggled it under her chin, he thought he saw another Peta. A woman with the mother instinct in her.

They were married not long afterwards. Peta went on with her job just as he went on with his. He didn't begrudge her the pleasure of running her kennels. They had a big country house, suitable for her hobby. Richard had money and Peta got all that she wanted. She was leading exactly the sort of life she liked. She rode and she hunted. And Richard, when he could get away, joined in her pursuits. Yes, from her point of view the marriage was an immense success.

But it was not altogether so from his. He found Peta all that he expected in a way. But he had made one big mistake. That mother-instinct which he had imagined was in her, did not exist — except for her puppies. She would nurse them on her lap, one, two, three

194

at a time. She would sit up all night with one of her hounds which was whelping. She wouldn't allow her kennel-maids to touch a new litter until she had inspected it. But babies she hated and quite frankly said so. She did not want a child of her own.

Richard Langden, on the other hand, wanted one badly. To him, marriage without children was rather a futile thing. It was all very well to have their big garden full of Irish wolf-hounds' puppies. They fulfilled Peta's requirements. But for him they couldn't take the place of children. It was absurd.

However, for two or three years Richard said nothing to Peta. He let her have her way. There were times when she looked such a kid herself that he wondered why he should expect motherhood of her. And they *were* happy.

But gradually that paternal instinct deepened — grew stronger than Richard's philosophies or his tolerance, and finally even stronger than his feelings for Peta. One evening after they had strolled round the kennels and locked up, he told her that he wanted a son.

She just looked at him for one frightened moment with her grey luminous eyes, then laughed and patted his shoulder.

'Oh no, darling. I just couldn't.'

He was gentle with her at first. He pleaded, argued. Finally he grew coldly angry.

'Aren't you being rather selfish?' he asked.

'But, darling, aren't *you*? . . . ' she parried, and was as cold and angry as he was.

'There must be something missing in you, Peta, if you don't want to have children.'

'Perhaps there is,' she said; 'and there it is, I wouldn't know what to do with a baby. I'd probably give it Lactol and Ruby mixture and puppy biscuit and kill it off.'

And she laughed. And she was still laughing when Richard turned on his heel and left her.

After that he did not open the subject with her again. Neither of them referred to it. Outwardly they were just as good friends. Occasionally they were lovers. But there was something missing between them. Something that made Peta a little uneasy, in spite of her relief that he was being 'sensible' about things. And he went about with a thwarted look in his eyes which was not altogether good to see.

A few months after that argument they went to Spain for a month's holiday. Peta was not keen on trusting her kennels, and some valuable dogs, to her maids, but Richard was on leave and was looking haggard, as though he was in need of a long vacation and she felt that she should take it with him.

They went to Andalusia. It was their first visit to Spain. A friend sent them to a *Pension* in a village which was a poem and an artist's dream; a nest of white cottages with yellow-tiled roofs, sombre mountains for a background, and a white-pebbled shore leading down to a sea that looked like blue crumpled silk.

The *Pension* itself had once been a castle and had white turrets, thick sunbaked walls with slits of windows, green spiky palm-trees like sentinels and a garden full of violent colour, the magenta of bougainvillaea and the pale purple of climbing passion-flowers. A place that surged with romance, a place with so much beauty that it took one's breath away, and Peta and Richard responded to it immediately.

Peta's one regret was that she hadn't a couple of her wolf-hounds with her. Richard agreed that she would look grand in her grey flannel slacks and white sweater, leading her dogs round the battlements. He left her a good deal these days and she became the idol of a party of young Oxford undergraduates who were out there, while Richard went off on his own. He liked to go up in the mountains and lie and think and dream. He was quieter than the Richard whom Peta had first married. A little less sociable. Not that she noticed it. She was too busy playing tennis and bathing with the boys. And she looked like one of them rather than a married woman.

It was during one of his lone mountain climbs on a donkey that Richard first saw the Spanish girl, Tirsa.

He had tethered his donkey to an olive-tree and was lying in the shade smoking, when he saw her coming down the dusty path which led up the mountainside. No doubt she came from Santa Grotia, the little village half a mile off.

She was about seventeen and, thought Richard, might have stepped out of a painting with her striped skirt, her little black-fringed shawl, the white flower behind one ear. She was a little on the plump side, but the man in Richard stirred at the sight of the pure oval face with its black lustrous eyes, and the voluptuous curve of her lips. She walked divinely, like most young girls of her race, swinging from the hips. He saw her not in the shabby peasant's clothes, but with long frilled skirt, a gay silk shawl flung over one white shoulder, a small foot arched, and castanets clicking in her hands.

Then that vision passed and he saw her quite differently, for she called a name, a small child ran out from behind a bush and she caught it up in her arms and covered its brown half-naked body with kisses. They were evidently sharing a joke for they screamed with laughter together.

It was a lovely sight. The madonna now rather than the dancer. And Richard, seeing the girl's warm olive cheek pressed against the dimpled one of the child, felt an indefinable ache in his heart, and at the same time there flashed through his mind a queer recollection of Peta when he had first met her at the dog-show, Peta caressing one of her puppies. Both women had worn that same rapt, tender look. Then his thoughts of Peta became bitter and angry. Love for a puppy! Faugh! It was utterly unnatural!

The Spanish girl had seen him now and was smiling in the friendly manner of her race. He jumped to his feet and gave her a greeting in Spanish, which he spoke fluently.

'*Buenos dias*,' he said to her. 'What a beautiful day it is!'

She kept hold of the child and answered shyly: '*Bueno, señor*. What a day, indeed!'

He induced her to sit down and talk to him and introduce him to the child. It was her little sister, and they came, as he imagined, from Santa Grotia. Tirsa was her name and she looked after half a dozen children. Her mother was ailing and Tirsa had to cook and sew, scold and caress the whole family in her mother's name.

Richard found her quaint and talkative. He let her ramble on, whilst all that was beauty-loving in him revelled in the perfection of her movements. She had exquisite hands, beautifully kept for a peasant-girl. Of course she had no brains, he thought. She was just a half-civilized little animal. In an English drawing-room beside a quick-witted, cultured woman like Peta, for instance, she would appear common and stupid. But physically she was perfection and there was something rather beautiful in her natural uncomplaining acceptance of her hard lot.

He asked her what she hoped for in the future. She answered without hesitation, a good husband and many children if sweet Jesus and the Saints were willing to hear her prayers.

Richard, who was showing his watch to Tirsa's enraptured little sister, gave her a covert look.

'So you want children, do you, Tirsa?'

'*Sí, señor*. Is it not natural?'

Again he thought of Peta, and a sudden hatred welled up in him. A hatred not of her, personally, but of her attitude towards life and of those damned dogs which took the place of her children.

Yes, it was natural, he told Tirsa. She

was right and he admired her. He respected her views.

Before they parted he gave the child a five-*peseta* piece and told Tirsa that he would come up to the mountains again and hoped to see her. She gave him a soft look from her velvety eyes and said that she would very much like to see him again. To her he was a grand, handsome Englishman with much money and a sad look which she did not understand, but which appealed to all that was feminine in her.

Peta, who was thoroughly enjoying her Spanish holiday, was in the best of spirits that evening, but Richard was quiet and even taciturn, and when she reproached him for being a wet-blanket he turned and snapped at her — a thing which he had never done in his life before.

'What's bitten you, darling?' she asked, wide-eyed.

'Nothing that you'd understand,' was his short reply. And then, because he knew that she mattered more than anything in the world and that he would have given years off his life to make her into the ideal of his imagination, he added: 'Sorry, Peta. I'm a bit off colour . . . '

He left her to dance with the boys. But she did not enjoy herself much. She was realizing now that Richard had been 'off colour' for a long time. They weren't happy like they used to be. It gave her food for thought.

And Richard went back to his beloved mountains. Back to the moonlight which poured down from a sky of large bright stars which were larger and brighter than any he had seen. A glorious night with scarcely a breath of wind stirring the olives. The brown twisted trunks and limbs of the cork trees threw grotesque shadows on the stubbly grass which was still hot from the day's sun, and the lights from the village twinkled and danced through the darkness.

Richard walked to Santa Grotia. He wondered if he would find Tirsa. He did find her, with a flower in her hair as usual, this time a scarlet one, a red shawl and some cheap blue beads round her neck. She was strolling down the narrow street flanked with crazy little cottages which were like an illustration from a fairy-tale in the moonlight. And Tirsa herself had a fairy-like beauty. She was with another girl, but when she saw Richard, Tirsa left her friend and joined the Englishman. Her eyes shone with an excitement which flowed also in Richard's veins. She said that she had been wondering whether she would see him again.

Richard, staid, sensible though he was, found himself responding to that arch flattery and asking if she had *wanted* to see him. Whereupon Tirsa blushed and said: '*Sí, señor,*' in a voice which held all the seduction of the ages.

They left the village together and went further up the mountainside where it was dark and quiet and there were only the radiant stars to look upon them.

And three days later — the tragedy!

Peta was lying on her bed enjoying an after-lunch siesta when one of the Oxford boys came running into her room with a white face and said: 'Mrs Langden, will you come at once? I think something has happened.'

Peta knew that it was Richard. For a moment she felt sick and giddy and the world stood still for her. The Oxford boy could tell her nothing except that Richard had just been brought in by a couple of donkey-boys and laid in his own room, and that someone had fetched the retired English doctor who was amongst the visitors in the *Pension*.

A moment later Peta was kneeling beside the bed in Richard's room which was opposite hers wondering whether he was going to die. He was not a pretty sight. His grey flannels were torn and disordered, his collar ripped off, his face swollen, covered with blood. The doctor was engaged in stanching a flow from a wound between his shoulder-blades, a knife-wound which, she afterwards learned, had missed a vital part by half an inch.

She called his name wildly. He opened his eyes and looked up at her and said: 'It was you all the time . . . *it was you . . . not her!* . . . '

That meant nothing to Peta just then, and for many days afterwards it meant nothing, because Richard lay in a hospital in Malaga between life and death. But the time came when he was well enough to explain. She sat by his side, very still and grim, for Peta, hearing what he had to say.

He had received that knife-wound trying to defend himself against a murderous attack of a Spaniard who worked in a vineyard in Santa Grotia. The man was the sweetheart of a girl named Tirsa. He had been suspicious and followed them. He had found Tirsa in Richard's arms and had tried to kill him.

It was no good lying, Richard said. He had no wish to lie. He had been unfaithful and he admitted it. He had made love to Tirsa and deserved what had happened to him.

Peta, hurt and bewildered, cried: 'But why, Dick, why, when I thought you and I were such good friends — good lovers, too?'

He told her, then, that Tirsa had stood for something more than passion — something outside it. *For motherhood.* She loved little children. She had wanted a child. She had wanted to give *him* one. She had said so with frank paganism. And something in him had broken, something that had been there for a very long while. He had taken her, giving way to an instinct as strong and old as the world itself. Only when that mad tornado of feeling had passed had he realized his folly.

He offered his apologies to Peta. Offered her her freedom, anything that she wanted. There was nothing else left for him to do, he said.

But something in Peta broke, also. She wept bitterly with her face in her hands like an ashamed boy. And she said: 'It's my fault. I see now it's all my fault. The girl was generous but I've been mean. It's I who ought to apologize to you, Dick. I don't want to be free, unless, of course, you wish to marry this girl.'

That wasn't what he wished at all. It was out of the question. He had never loved anybody but Peta. Tirsa remained, however — a grave responsibility — for she had been abandoned by her lover and turned out by her family and was at the moment living with an old aunt in a mean street in Malaga, giving in return her services in the fish-shop which the old woman ran.

During the months that followed, whilst Richard lay in hospital, slowly recovering from his wound, it was Peta who went to the fish-shop, saw Tirsa, gave her money, and offered to do what she could for her. Tirsa was an expectant mother. The mother of Richard's child! A bitter pill for Peta to swallow, but she swallowed it because she knew that it was not Richard's folly but her own egotism which lay at the root of the evil.

The Spanish girl did not expect the Señor to marry her, but she was glad of the Señora's help. She did not see Richard again. And a couple of months later, when Richard was strong enough to go back to his job, it was Peta who saw that Tirsa was provided for and left not in the degradation of the fish-shop, but in a home run by Spanish nuns where they assured Peta that Tirsa would have every attention.

During the months that followed at home, Richard was in a state of nerves and misery, but Peta was extraordinarily patient with him. She went on as usual working in her kennels and seemingly engrossed in her dogs. But in her way she thought as much as Richard about that girl in Malaga.

In due course the expected cable came to say that Tirsa had given birth to a daughter. But quite unexpectedly it added that the young mother was not going to live. In spite of coming of healthy peasant stock, complications had set in, and a further cable twenty-four hours later informed the Langdens of her death.

Richard went to pieces. He blamed himself for the girl's death. But Peta took charge of the situation. It was Peta who went out to Malaga, travelling by air and by train, arriving in time to see poor Tirsa's beauty laid in a cold grave, hidden away from men's sight for ever.

And it was Peta who received the bundle which the nuns laid in her arms and looked at the tiny face, and touched, half fearfully, the black down on the tiny head, and realized that the baby was sweet to hold . . . as sweet as one of her puppies. It made the same sort of funny little cooing noise. The eyes, they were ridiculously Dick's blue eyes in Tirsa's brown face.

Peta struggled with her tears, and in a half-shamed way she bent and put her lips against the baby's head, and whispered: 'I mustn't give you Lactol — or puppy biscuit, must I? I'll have to learn how to run another sort of kennel now, I suppose . . . '

She brought the baby back to England in the care of a Spanish nurse.

Richard Langden, returning from his work that evening looking haggard and feeling wretched, knew by the frenzied barking in the kennels that Peta had returned. The wolfhounds were baying their welcome.

But it was not to the kennels that Peta led him for the usual inspection. It was to a room at the top of the house where an infant lay in a cot, contentedly sucking a fist. For a paralysed instant Richard stared down into the blue eyes of his baby daughter. Then he went down on his knees at Peta's feet. What was said between them need not be repeated or even imagined here.

And that was the story of the Langdens. Tragic in its way, even though the ending was a happy one. For, so my doctor friend informed me that afternoon in the Spanish Club as we watched the Langdens, Richard could never quite forget that he had made two women suffer and one had paid the price of her life for giving way to his impulses on that Spanish mountainside.

'So the girl is not hers,' I said. 'But the boy . . . ?'

'Ah!' said the doctor. 'The boy came a couple of years later. You see, Peta Langden sold her kennels. She found that she was rather interested in the rearing of her adopted baby. And I think she decided that it was high time she gave her husband a son.'

'She's been rather grand,' I said.

'On the whole women are grand,' said the doctor.

I looked across the room at Peta Langden and did not argue the point.

Interlude

The moment they saw each other at the Hills' cocktail party which was held at the Dorchester, they were mutually attracted. Pilot-Officer Tim Wenbury was bored to death by young 'lovelies' who floated round him regularly at The Officers' Club where he was stationed. He was struck at once by the grace and poise of the woman. Besides being beautiful she was so exquisitely aloof and serene and she looked intelligent. As soon as he saw that the cocktail glass in her hand was empty, he walked across the lounge to her and said: 'Let me get you another drink.'

Veronica Ellis had already singled him out from the other young men in the hotel. What was it she liked about him? His youth, perhaps. He had a delightful boy's head, a gay, impudent smile, and a way of looking at a woman.

She judged him to be in the early twenties. She had found out from her hostess that he was in the RAF, stationed near London at the moment, but shortly going north as an instructor.

'I'd love another pink gin,' she said, and handed him her glass. Until that moment, when she smiled up into his eyes, she had been finding the party dull and the lounge hot. But now she was interested; glad, too, that she was wearing that black suit by Digby Morton (it was divinely cut), and that she had remembered Jean Patou's *Amour-Amour* and had put some on her hair which was crowned with a ridiculous little hat made of feathers. The hat merged into the black of her head and hid some of those silver threads that were beginning to weave into the inexorable pattern of age.

Pilot-Officer Wenbury came back with a drink for her and one for himself. He sat on the arm of her chair and they talked. He hurled eager questions at her which she answered.

She had been in London for the last few months. Yes, she lived in the country — her home was really in Suffolk. But she had shut up her country house and taken a flat in Town. Alone, yes, quite. (She saw no reason to add details of the domestic circle out of which she had escaped.)

Tim Wenbury obviously thought that she was little more than a contemporary of his. He talked about taking her out to dance. He would be in London for another week. She *must* come.

She nodded and smiled and said nothing about George, her husband. (At this moment, George was probably playing bridge in the hotel at Harrogate, to which he had retired with a lot of other elderly invalids like himself.) Nor about Alan, her twenty-year-old son who was at Oxford, and that tall lanky daughter of hers, Elizabeth Ann, still at Cheltenham.

For years Veronica had not been permitted to forget that she was a wife and mother. Lately she had been restless.

Romance, that exquisite thrill so essential to a woman's happiness, seemed to have gone right out of her life. One could be gay and courageous about George losing money and all of them 'cutting down' these hard days — but to grow old was rather depressing. She enjoyed letting this young airman treat her as though she were a girl; she reacted like one to the nonsense that he talked.

He asked her to dine with him tonight. She accepted it because it seemed the most agreeable thing in the world to do. Tomorrow he was busy all day, he said, but suggested that he could be with her by eight o'clock. Well, why not? She was her own mistress. George wasn't here to follow her about, and the children weren't around to put her, metaphorically, in a corner with her knitting. There was glamour about the way Tim Wenbury looked at her, and a wild stirring of her blood such as she had not felt for years, all because a good-looking boy said: 'You are the most desperately lovely thing I have ever seen. Why haven't I met you before?'

She laughed and said: 'Idiot.'

And fell to thinking what she'd wear tonight. That new slim-line green Christian Dior, her most expensive and clever frock, which made her hips look so slight? Or the old red which was divine for her warm white skin.

That night Veronica and Tim Wenbury dined and danced at The Bagatelle. The party was being a rapturous success. Tim was head over ears in love with her and she felt ridiculously flattered and almost afraid of the response that his ardour awoke in her. She could not believe that she was the same Veronica who led a conventional 'county' existence in Suffolk, ordering special food for George, worrying about the children and going more *passé* every day.

Tonight she was young and a goddess, and a boy, little older than her own son, adored her.

When he drove her home, Tim kissed Veronica on the lips and the throat and said: 'That scent of yours! Gosh, if I never saw you again I should remember it. But, Veronica, you're going to see me again. You'll come out with me again tomorrow night, won't you?'

She knew that she should say 'no'. She knew that it was mad and dangerous to fan a fire like this, with George and Alan and Elizabeth Ann in the background; *And* the fact that she was nearly forty-five to make the whole thing seem a little ridiculous. Sooner or later Tim would find out about her age and her family.

All that next day, working feverishly at the office, she admonished herself: 'Go and write to George. Send Alan all the news he is waiting for. Remember that Elizabeth is sitting for her music-exam and you ought to be anxious about it. Remember that both wings of hair over your two ears are white, *absolutely white.*'

Yet the whole of life's enthusiasms and splendours were concentrated for Veronica into one hour that night when she came face to face in the lounge with an eager boy who looked at her with his adoring eyes and took her once again out to dine and dance.

At dawn, when London was quiet and the stars had dimmed, they drove along the Embankment. It was not fair, Veronica told herself. It was much too lovely beside the grey, misty river, with the dawn breaking across the sky and the great Battersea Power House standing there like a splendid modern etching, defying the baroque beauties of the Victorian monuments. It was quiet and cool and lovely, and Tim Wenbury's arms and lips were the arms and lips of an ardent boy, difficult to resist.

When he declared that now that he had found her — the only woman he could ever love — he would never let her go, she tried to think, idiotically, about telling George that this was a serious affair. Then, with a remnant of sanity she managed to elude Tim's caresses for a few moments, and made him talk about himself.

He had been in the Royal Air Force since he left public school. Yes, he was a 'regular', not a National Serviceman. He had a young brother at Oxford (that made her heart shake with the memory of Alan). They had both gone skiing together in Switzerland in St Moritz last winter. He adored ski-ing. She must ski with him one day, he said, on his next winter leave. (Another heart-shake for Veronica. It was a sport which she had never cared for and she was too old to begin now!) Tim went on enthusing about winter sports. Then he said suddenly: 'Good lord, I've just remembered I met an awfully nice fellow out in Davos — the same name as yourself — Ellis. Alan Ellis. Crazy about flying; means to join up when he comes down from Oxford. I promised to try and call on his people when I got home. Then I was posted to Germany for a time and I forgot all about it. But now I remember. I wonder if you know the Ellis family. Have you a cousin Alan, or something?'

Veronica Ellis bent her head. Tim was still holding her hands, but he could not see the sick look in her eyes. She whispered: 'No.'

Tim continued: 'He said I would like his mother, particularly. He adored her. As a matter of fact I had a letter a week or two ago from Alan — written in Oxford. Made me laugh. He said: 'The old girl's damned decent to me about everything but hates the idea of me joining the Air Force. You must look her up and try to persuade her that it's OK!' That's the worst of mothers, Veronica, isn't it? No matter how charming they are, they are apt to be fools about their sons. What does she want Alan to do? Be a solicitor or something, I suppose, so he can live at home. And he has set his heart on the Air Force. These elderly women do get silly notions, don't they? Fancy being scared of flying these days.'

Silence. Veronica, her face very white in the moonlight, looked down at the brown rippling waters of the Thames.

Her eyes were stricken. She thought: 'God! I've made a fool of myself. *Elderly women — the old girl!*'

Those words bit like acid into her. She felt she could hardly bear the echo of them.

'Darling,' said Tim, 'what is it?'

Veronica said: 'I'm getting cold. Will you take me home?'

'Of course. But we'll meet again tomorrow night.'

Then she gave him a cool strange smile and said: 'I think it will be best if we don't meet any more, my dear!'

He stared at her, puzzled.

'But why — in heaven's name why?'

'I can't tell you.'

And she couldn't. She never could tell him. And she must *never* meet him again, either alone or with her son. It would never do for Tim to have a second introduction to *the old girl*.

Black Fan

1

The ship moved slowly into the docks.

The charming-looking man with the brown hair, which had just a touch of grey over the ears, was leaning over the ship's rails, looking through half-closed eyes at the crowd on the quay. He was smiling. But his fine-cut lips had an ironic twist to them.

He turned to the fair woman who stood beside him. 'Well, there's one thing I do know . . . Roddy Hamilton won't find a soul he knows in that crowd!'

Vanessa Lane turned and looked at him. Her own lips were unmistakably sad, like those strange turquoise blue eyes of hers into which most men wanted to look more than once. And during the long journey from Mombasa, Rodney Hamilton had spent most of his time looking into them. The scandal-loving wives had remarked cattily that it was 'a shame' that Mrs Lane should capture the best-looking man on board. And the unmarried girls had even more cattily suggested that it was always the 'married' ones who were the worst! In fact, it had been taken for granted that Mr Hamilton and Mrs Lane had had a flaming affair — although they had been strangers when they embarked.

Thought Vanessa: 'How little they know about us. The only truth in it is that *I* am in love with Roddy. But he is in love with his wife and she has run away from him and he is going back to an empty flat. Every day ... every evening since we met he has been telling me that life is finished for him because he has lost beautiful Eve, and from what I can gather she is a hard, selfish little brute who has taken all she can get and given nothing in return. A wife who couldn't be bothered to join her husband in Kenya because she didn't want to leave London. Now she has met somebody with a lot more money — somebody who doesn't have to work for his living. And she has gone with him. And Roddy is alone. Roddy worshipped her!'

She knew just what he was feeling and thinking as the ship came alongside the quay. The sickness of his despair; of his wounded pride; his dread of the loneliness. She knew so much about it. She had listened to his story night after night ... about his little flat near Sloane Square and the fun he and Eve had had furnishing it five years ago. How proud he had been of her beauty. How well she danced. The dreams he had had of staying permanently in London now that his work in Kenya had been handed over to another man. He was not a rich man, but he had a new job waiting for him and, though Vanessa didn't know the details, it seemed that the new job would bring in enough to keep the normal wife very well. But not enough for Eve.

Vanessa knew even more than Roddy had told her. She had had a drink or two on board with a friend of his and he had told Vanessa that Eve Hamilton was as beautiful as a dream — and as empty. And what a good chap Roddy was, and how he had been saving — for her. Cutting down the drink, cutting out cars and expensive trips so that he could pile up the LSD for when he got home.

How rotten! Vanessa thought, to get home and find nothing waiting for you except a divorce.

He hadn't even a family of his own — only a couple of old aunts with whom he had had no recent contact. She hated to think of him — absolutely alone tonight.

And she hated to think of her own loneliness.

Hers was equally a depressing home-coming. Not that her grief was as fresh and raw as his; nor in its way as bitter or frustrating. She was alone, but Bill had left her in quite a different way. Two years ago . . . unwillingly, he had slipped away into the Unknown, the victim of a rare and painful malady which he had contracted while in India.

She had loved Bill very much and he had loved her. Theirs had been a perfect marriage, except that there had been no children — a great grief to them both. But one couldn't have everything, and she had often looked around at all the mistaken marriages, the broken romances, the hectic futile love-affairs in the various parts of the world in which they had lived . . . and thought how lucky they were.

Ten years they had together. She had married him when she was twenty-one and then he had left her. And because of her memories of the intolerable pain and aching void . . . remembering the countless things shared . . . the love and life which had become a habit . . . oh, she knew it all! Right from the start she had been drawn to Roddy Hamilton. She had felt capable of walking with him down that grim road of loss and misery. Only, in a way, his suffering must be worse because death is kinder than disillusionment.

Vanessa had been working since Bill died. At thirty-two she had not found it easy to start again but she needed to earn something in addition to her pension and someone had offered her a good job in Nairobi.

She had been out there for two years and met many men who wanted to make love to her . . . one or two whom she had cared enough about to respond to in a mild fashion. But nobody who made her heart beat really fast. Nobody whom she had felt could ever come up to the idealistic memory of the man she had lost.

Until she met Roddy Hamilton.

They had liked each other from the very start. And perhaps she had been more drawn to him than to any other man in recent years, because of his story. She had been first of all intrigued — then deeply sorry for him — and never bored, even though he spoke so often of the other woman. Finally she fell in love . . .

He hadn't even kissed her. Once

— on one of those magic nights of moonlight, sitting on a secluded part of the boat-deck, away from the crowd of officers and wives who were playing tombola in the dining saloon . . . he had taken her hand. Holding it, he had told her that her sweetness and sympathy had helped a lot . . . made a difference to what he had expected to be a painful and lonely voyage home. He had thanked her. He had said: 'Life hasn't been very kind to either of us, Vanessa. And it must be worse for you. It's always worse for a woman.'

Then, when she had dared to speak . . . to smile so that he should not know how her heartbeats shook her body . . . she had asked him what he meant to do, and he had said: Sell up the flat and spend all the money he had saved for Eve in an effort to forget her.

That was all. What more could one expect of a man who was still in love with the woman he had lost.

This morning . . . a grey morning, cold after the heat of Africa . . . Vanessa looked at Roddy's pain-twisted mouth, saw the old devil of torment in his eyes and wondered that he did not guess the torments that lay in her own heart — for *him*.

It was a good thing they had reached port, she told herself a little wildly. She could not go on seeing Roddy in this close association and not give herself away.

The big ship had come to a standstill. Over the tannoy a voice was blaring orders. And then ... '*There are messages in the orderly room for Mr Rodney Hamilton ... Mrs Smith ... Captain O'Connor.*'

Vanessa forced a smile at her tall companion.

'That's you, Roddy.'

He had thrust a pipe into his mouth and jerked one shoulder in a nervous way.

'I shall be glad to be quit of all this discipline, won't you?'

'I've quite enjoyed my voyage home,' she said simply.

Now he forgot the message waiting for him and looked down into the unusual blue of Vanessa's large eyes. What a pretty woman she was, he thought. Still quite a girl, and at times quite beautiful with that silver-gilt hair; ash-blonde they called it. Eve had had hair like that. When he had first seen Vanessa walk into the dining saloon he had thought how like her hair was to Eve's. But nothing else. Vanessa was a widow, mature, poised, and a little taller than he liked most women to be. A little thinner, too. Poor dear! It was obvious that she had been through the mill. As though the loss of her husband had quenched the flame that must have burned in her long ago. But Eve was small and rounded and exquisitely made for men's desiring. With a ripe, red mouth, pouting lips which seemed to ask for the world and make a man long to give it to her in one long kiss.

Somehow it had never entered his head to kiss Vanessa's cool coral-tinted mouth.

Yet, suddenly he became conscious of the fact that their friendship had grown to mean more than a little to him since he came on this ship. That he would miss her — her calm voice and quiet sympathy.

She was the same age as himself — widowed — wasted. She ought to marry again . . .

'What about your message, Roddy?' her quiet voice interrupted his train of thought.

He nodded, sighed and walked away.

Twisting her hands together, Vanessa looked through a sudden mist of tears at the crowd on the quay. She wished she had not come home for this leave.

She had nothing to look forward to except seeing her old father and mother, who lived a life of retreat in their backwater, a tiny cottage in St Ives. Vanessa's father had been in the Merchant Navy. She had been born late in life. Both parents were now over seventy — out of touch with the modern world. She had come home to see them, but she couldn't stay long in the tiny cottage. She had grown away from it — from them. She had had a home of her own for so long. Bill's death had taken it, and everything else from her. After a few days in St Ives, she would make a round of visits to old friends, and then . . . back to Nairobi and her job. She would probably never see Roddy Hamilton again. He had said that once his divorce was in progress, instead of taking up his post in London, he meant to ask for a job in the Far East — as far away from England and Eve as he could get.

Vanessa bit hard on her lower lip. She wanted, badly, to cry. She had not felt so unhappy since Bill died.

She heard Roddy's voice behind her.

'A message for me from my wife.'

Vanessa did not look at Roddy — afraid that he might see the moisture in her eyes.

'Is it . . . good news?'

He laughed in a hard way.

'Just a choice greeting. Welcome

239

home and please get on with the divorce because the man she wants to marry may be going to South America, and she wants to go with him. For a moment I thought perhaps she had changed her mind. I was a fool.'

As usual Vanessa forgot her own pain in the effort to help Roddy conquer his.

'I'm sorry, my dear, but don't let it get you down. Life holds much for you yet. You're so very nice . . . ' Her voice trailed away.

He gave a bitter smile.

'Nice . . . is that it? Have I been too nice to *her*? Perhaps women appreciate men who kick them around a bit?'

'Oh no, no! Don't be so cynical . . . don't let it make you any different. It's just that you weren't suited to each other.'

He said: 'Where are *you* going tonight? What are *you* doing?'

She stammered. 'I . . . don't know. Nothing much. My people live in Cornwall. I'm going down there tomorrow. I shall spend tonight in Town. I have a room booked in a hotel.'

Rodney Hamilton fingered the letter which his wife had written him from Paris — crushing it between his fingers. He looked down into Vanessa's sorrowful turquoise eyes. He said: 'Why shouldn't we make an evening of it together? I'll take you out to dinner. We might dance. Wouldn't it be nicer than being alone . . . for both of us?'

She had to sit tight on all her emotions as she smiled up at the brown, fine-drawn face which had become so unbelievably dear to her in such a short time.

'I think it would be very much better,' she said, in a breathless voice.

They travelled on the boat-train together. At the station they parted; she to go to her hotel in Knightsbridge, and he to his flat — the two-roomed luxury flat in an expensive block, which Roddy had struggled so hard to keep going for Eve because she liked it.

Vanessa had said: 'Must you go there? It's bound to be full of painful memories.'

But he had to face them some time, he had said, so why not at once. Tomorrow he would pack up and finish with it.

He telephoned her a few hours later. 'What are you wearing tonight, Vanessa?' he asked. 'I'd like to give you a shoulder spray.'

The abrupt question rather took her breath away.

'I've only got one dinner dress — the one I wore on the boat the night we danced. Black-pleated chiffon.'

'I remember it,' Roddy said. 'You looked lovely.'

Her pleasure in his praise lasted only a few seconds. He added on a note of despair: 'I've had a hellish few hours, Vanessa. I ought never to have come here. If you could see how it all looks! — how she left it — in chaos! Tidiness was never one of her strong points, and I'm afraid I've been sitting here just looking at it all, with a whisky in one hand and a cigarette in the other — like a dumb, damned fool!'

His voice cracked into a laugh that jarred her.

Vanessa said in a strong, clear voice: 'Listen. I'm coming right round, Roddy. You need a female to put things right. Hold on. Wait for me. I'm just finishing dressing . . .'

She never quite knew afterwards what impulse it was that sent her rushing round to Roddy's flat that evening. Nor how much more deeply she would feel the whole thing, when she saw the welcome Eve Hamilton had left her husband. It was unbelievably chaotic and dusty. The final gesture of utter egoism and thoughtlessness. And Roddy standing there, still with his whisky in one hand and his cigarette in the other, looking blindly at his ruined home. Eve had taken her personal luggage with her. The bare furniture remained, and a litter of paper and boxes, and all the things that had belonged to Roddy.

Vanessa felt sick with pity for him. The bedroom seemed particularly tragic.

Much of Eve's personality lingered there. Half-finished jars and bottles of make-up . . . an unwanted dress left hanging in the cupboard, a foolish, gay little hat with a broken feather, on the floor. And on the big, low bed, a pair of gloves and a black lace fan.

Slowly Vanessa moved forward and picked up the fan.

'I wonder why she didn't take that!'

Roddy had followed her into the room and she heard him laugh. He tossed down his drink and turned down the glass on the palm of his hand.

'Turn down the empty glass!' he quoted. '*Finito! No more. Too late. Farewell!*'

She turned to him. 'Stop being dramatic and go and get dressed, Roddy,' she said in a low tone.

He pulled himself together.

'You're right. I'm just a little drunk. Maybe there's an excuse. Maybe not! But you're very good to me, Vanessa, and I'm grateful. Go and sit down next door, my dear, and mix yourself a drink. I won't be long. Incidentally you look charming . . . '

She flushed and turned away.

'Oh, go and get dressed!' she almost snapped the words.

When he returned to her, shaven, dark hair smooth, dressed in the white tuxedo which brought back all her memories of the voyage home (it made his face look so brown), she had tidied the room. She looked flushed and younger than he had ever seen her. And he noticed that she was holding the black lace fan — Eve's fan.

'Do you like that thing?' he asked.

'I think it's exquisite.'

'Eve bought it in an antique shop when she was in Madrid. She's left it, so take it. It seems to go with your dress, Vanessa. It's a warm night, and you may need it. We're going to dance. We're going to dance the whole evening. Eve didn't like dancing with me. But you do . . . *you do, don't you?*'

She moved towards him.

'I love it, Roddy.'

'Let's go,' he said. 'No, don't put the

fan down. *Take it*. She didn't want it. She never used it, that I can remember, from the first day that it was bought.'

Vanessa did not argue. He seemed to want her to have the fan. She didn't really wish to have it because it had belonged to the girl who had hurt him so profoundly. But it seemed to give him some satisfaction to see her using it.

Once they were out of the flat his mood changed. He became a gay and attractive companion. She could not stop him spending money. An orchid to pin on her evening bag. Special flowers on her table; tawny tiger lilies, which she had not seen for years . . . champagne . . . a special dinner. And dancing . . . Every dance, tirelessly. A languorous waltz, a gay Samba, laughter and jesting and no more mention of Eve. No nostalgic memories. Only themselves.

Vanessa had not been so happy for years . . . or so wretched. Wretched because she knew that tomorrow it must all end.

They went on to a night-club. In the taxi driving slowly home through the Park in the small hours of the summer morning, Roddy kissed her. For a moment she clung to him, feeling utterly fulfilled and yet full of an intolerably painful ecstasy as she felt his passionate kiss upon her upturned mouth.

He whispered: 'Forgive me for losing my head a little . . . you're so damned sweet. Any man would find you a temptation, Vanessa. Darling, kind, generous Vanessa!'

The little black lace fan that had belonged to Eve Hamilton slid from her hand on to the floor of the taxi. Her two slim hands locked round his neck. He said: 'You're going the hell of a long way away tomorrow. Will you come back? Will you come out with me again? I need you, Vanessa.'

With all her soul in her eyes, she answered: 'You know I will come any time you want me to, Roddy . . .'

It was he who picked up the fan and

gave it back to her when the taxi stopped outside her hotel.

'Keep it,' he said, 'as a memento of tonight, when you saved my reason.'

She wept herself sick and blind in the dawn, remembering those words. She had saved him from his own despair. But that was all, and he was still in love with the beautiful young wife who had walked out on him.

She went down to St Ives that day, feeling that it was the end of the world.

2

Within a week of seeing her old parents, Vanessa was filled with restlessness and a quite crazy desire to see what was happening to Roddy Hamilton, from whom she had not heard a word since the night of their return.

The black lace fan went with her. It held for her now an almost sinister fascination. It had belonged to the other woman . . . his wife . . . but she had left it behind and he had given it to her. And when she looked at it, she thought of the long emotional hours of dancing with Roddy, and of that long embrace in the taxi. The kisses that had meant heaven to her, but for him only a momentary release from hell.

She rang him up at his flat. There was no answer. She wandered around London in a mood of discontent and restlessness and then . . . on an impulse

. . . called at the flat in person, just before half past six that evening . . . He had been out all day. He might now be back. Surely he would not have got rid of the place so quickly?

The front door was opened by a slim girl with the face of a beautiful spoilt child, and a sophisticated black dress, cut daringly low. Vanessa's heart stopped beating. She knew before the girl spoke, that this was Roddy's wife.

'I . . . I'm a friend of Mr Hamilton's . . . ' Vanessa began to stammer.

The girl said in a friendly way: 'Oh yes, come in. You're just in time for a drink. I'm Eve Hamilton. Roddy's away on business. I was in Paris when he got home, but I spoke to him on the telephone. I'm expecting him back tomorrow. Did you meet abroad?'

'Yes. I . . . I'm Mrs Lane . . . I . . . we travelled home on the same boat. I . . . just thought I'd look him up.'

Eve Hamilton looked Vanessa up and down. A woman older than herself. Quite chic, she thought. Poor old

250

Roddy's type. She wondered idly if this was a girlfriend of his. Well, she couldn't blame Roddy if he wanted soothing. At the same time, things weren't working out quite Eve's way. In fact, not at all! Vanessa's arrival was at the psychological moment when Eve was bored, and a little anxious, and wanting someone to talk to.

She insisted upon Vanessa going into the sitting-room and having a drink.

Vanessa watched her in silent dismay. What had happened? She knew nothing. She could only guess dimly that Roddy's wife had decided to return to him. Heavens! How perfectly beautiful she was, except for that discontented droop of the petulant mouth. And the obvious absence of any heart. She was hard . . . hard through and through. She had a hard voice and hard eyes. But physically she was flawless, and wore that silver gilt hair of hers like a cap, smooth and shining, cut in a straight fringe across the pencilled brows.

It wasn't long before Vanessa knew

what had happened. Eve was not reserved. She had none of Vanessa's dislike of showing her feelings in public. What feelings she had, she aired instantly and with a rather childish desire to impress. Vanessa was a complete stranger but there was nothing, shortly, that she did not know about Eve's attitude towards life and her marriage.

She plied Vanessa with sherry and cigarettes. She praised Vanessa's dress. She said: 'No wonder Roddy liked you. You're so distinguished. Just his type. I never was, and neither was he mine really. We were mad ever to get married.'

With pain catching her by the throat, Vanessa cried: 'But he adores the ground you walk on.'

Eve shrugged her shoulders. 'More's the pity. Roddy is a dear, but I couldn't adore *him*. He's too old for me — and too quiet. I like someone young and a little crazy . . . '

And then Vanessa heard all about the

South American millionaire playboy for whom she had left poor Roddy. Why hadn't she carried on with her plans? Because dear Marco had let her down. Not his fault, of course. But he already had a wife who was a Catholic and he found that he could not get a divorce. He had been heart-broken — and so had she, Eve. So she had come back to Roddy. She knew that he would forgive her. He always forgave her everything.

She laughed. An empty laugh like the tinkle of a bell. Vanessa froze as she heard it. She sat silent, smoking, listening . . . unable to tear herself away, although she wanted to rush out of the flat, out of the sight of this girl who held a decent man like Roddy in the hollow of her greedy little hand.

There followed further chatter from Eve. She was inordinately vain. She seemed to want to tell Roddy's 'girlfriend' about her conquests, the other men in her life. The other little affairs. And the affairs that she hoped for in the future.

'I could never settle down with Roddy. One day — who knows — Marco's wife may die and he'll come back for me . . . Why not?'

Another tinkling laugh; hard brilliant eyes laughing under the devastating, long lashes.

Vanessa stubbed her cigarette in an ashtray and rose to her feet. She was shaken. To *this*, Roddy was coming back tomorrow. To this bundle of egotism . . . a lovely heartless creature who had left him once, hurt him abominably and was prepared to do it all over again.

Somehow she managed to excuse herself and rush away from Eve Hamilton.

She hardly slept that night.

She knew now that she loved Roddy more than anything in the world. If Eve had loved him, she, Vanessa might have gone away feeling some kind of peace, and even satisfaction, for Roddy's sake, that the girl had decided to return to him. But the idea that Roddy's heart might be recaptured and then broken all over again appalled her.

She did not know what to do with the rest of her leave. She felt less than ever like visiting old friends. She loved being at St Ives with the old people, but they still treated her like a child, to be questioned and fussed over, which irked her. They did not seem able to remember that she had been married and was now a widow.

Breakfasting alone in her hotel that next morning, she realized forlornly what a lot she had staked on seeing Roddy Hamilton again. She was delighted and astonished when, just before lunch, he called in person to see her.

She fancied that he looked pale and harassed, and that there were new, tired lines round his eyes. After their greeting, they sat together in a quiet corner of the writing-room. It was one of those hot grey drenching mornings of summer, when London seemed to be a city of suffocation. Vanessa had ordered iced drinks. While they waited they smoked their cigarettes, regarding

each other with a curious embarrassment. Each, perhaps, remembering the
evening of a week ago.

Roddy said: 'I've just seen my wife.
She told me that you'd called at the flat
yesterday.'

Vanessa nodded, her cheeks burning.
'Was that indiscreet?'

'Not at all. I wanted very much to see
you. I fully intended to get in touch
with you myself, but I've been away
most of the week. I had to go out of
Town to see someone about my next
job. Eve telephoned me from Paris. You
know, of course, that she has come
back?'

Vanessa looked gravely at him. She
wished that her heart would not pound
and that her whole body would not
tremble with the agonizing delight of
seeing him again. She said: 'Yes, I know.
I . . . I'm so glad for you, Roddy. She is
. . . absolutely beautiful . . . ' Vanessa's
voice trailed away. She no longer looked
at him.

There was a curious expression in

Roddy Hamilton's own eyes, as he gazed at the bent fair head.

'Yes, she is very beautiful,' he said slowly, 'and I was once very much in love with her. *You* know what I felt.'

'Yes, I know.' (She was fastening on that significant word *once*.)

'Somehow, suddenly everything seems to have crashed. I was a bit off my rocker that first night when I got back to the flat. You know all about *that* too.'

Vanessa nodded. She knew . . . and her anguished heart rebelled against the thought that perhaps he had only drawn close to her and kissed her with such passionate tenderness because he had been so crazy, and not because he had really cared. Roddy went on speaking.

Everything had changed, he told her. It was as though he had woken up to the realization that he did not want his wife back, in the circumstances . . . knowing that she would have gone with that other man had the way been easier for her . . . that she had come back to him, her husband, only because she had been left in the lurch by the other man.

And yet, because he had once loved her so much, he could not refuse to take her back. If she wanted another chance, he felt he must give it to her. But he could not say frankly that he was happy about it.

He felt, he said, as though, while he had been abroad, he had built up an ideal of her which had never existed. He had never quite known how shallow, how cold she was. When he had first seen her this morning, for instance, she had refused to go out with him because she had a hair appointment and a fitting. That was all that their reunion meant to her.

Vanessa watched and listened, the old pity surging up in her heart. It hadn't taken him long to find out the truth this time. Poor Roddy! But because of his principles and his old love for Eve, he was willing to take her back again.

He talked to Vanessa for an hour. At the end of it he suddenly put out a hand and caught one of hers, pressing it tightly.

'What an egoist I am! All this has been about me. What about *you*!'

'Oh, I'm fine,' she said with a bright, hard smile.

He eyed her with sudden anxiety. The golden tan of the sun was still upon her, but her eyes looked deeply fatigued, and the exquisite blue of them brought vividly to mind the sweetness and beauty of this gentle, calm woman, who had been so extraordinarily kind to him.

Impulsively he said: 'I shall never forget our voyage home — nor the party we had in Town together. I've thought a lot about it. About you. If only she had been more like *you* — ' He broke off, dropped her hand and rose to his feet abruptly.

Vanessa also stood up. She hardly dared meet his gaze. So much had been left unsaid between them, yet what he had said was already too much. She was filled with the most bitter resentment against life and with a wild pagan wish that Eve Hamilton had never chosen to return.

'I must go,' she said in a strangled voice. 'I don't suppose we shall see each other again. Goodbye. Good luck, Roddy.'

The man's brows contracted. 'Must it be goodbye?'

'You have your wife and your own life to go back to now,' she reminded him.

He took a swift, regretful look at her. Once he had thought her too tall and too thin, because he had been blinded by the memory of Eve's petite and bewitching loveliness. Now, suddenly he thought this slender woman in the brown and white silk suit, with a brown wide-brimmed sailor hat on the fair, gracious head, more beautiful than Eve had ever been in her life. And he hated the thought of losing her. But he bowed his head to the inevitable.

Vanessa Lane walked out of the writing-room and out of his life.

Three days later he received a

registered parcel. It was the black lace fan. There was no message attached to it, but the box bore the postmark of *St Ives*. It did not need that to tell him that it had come from Vanessa. His face flushed under the tan, and his fingers gripped the fan so tightly that the delicate carved bone handle snapped suddenly in two. He gave a short laugh. It was as well that Eve had gone out and was not there to see — to sneer. But he did not throw the broken fan away. He put it into a private drawer of his own desk, and locked it up. Locked it away with his memories of a dear and lovely woman whose turquoise eyes had smiled at him with such infinite sweetness on the one night in his life when he had most needed a woman's understanding. He was left with those few memories of her, and an impossible hope for the future. These last few days had shown him how little his wife cared, and he knew that he could never feel the same way about her again.

3

Vanessa's leave was nearly up. She was due to return to Nairobi at the end of the first week in August.

She had enjoyed little of it. Everything seemed to have fallen flat after that first wildly exhilarating evening in London with Roddy Hamilton. She had not heard from him again and, beyond sending him the black fan, she had made no attempt to break what she considered a necessary silence.

That did not mean that she had forgotten him for a single moment, and it seemed to her that in these days the old sorrow and loss she had sustained by Bill's death had become a new sorrow. A new loss, in which the tall man with brown hair, silvered over the ears, and deep grey eyes, and a sense of humour and sympathy, was the main figure.

She had spent her time between her parents' home and her friends.

Forty-eight hours before she was due to fly back to Kenya, she went up to the usual hotel in London. She was due to dine that night with Bill's former CO and great friend — John Brande.

It was Colonel Brande who gave her the astounding and unexpected news.

After dinner, smoking a cigar over the coffee, he said:

'Wasn't it you, Vass, my dear, who told me that you came back on a ship this summer with Rodney Hamilton?'

Vanessa nodded. Roddy's name woke far too many nostalgic memories. Why good heavens, she thought, tonight she was even wearing the very same black chiffon dress she had worn when she dined with Roddy.

'Yes,' she nodded. 'It was I who told you. His wife had run away from him at the time. But she has since come back.'

'Ah!' said Colonel Brande. 'That's the thing . . . I met a chap at the Club yesterday who knows Hamilton, and he was telling me the tragic thing that happened to that girl.'

Vanessa looked at her old friend with two startled blue eyes. 'What happened?'

'She was killed in a car smash about a fortnight ago.'

The restaurant went out of focus for Vanessa for a moment. Her heart almost stopped beating. She whispered: 'Eve Hamilton . . . *dead?*'

'So this chap told me. It seems to have been a bit of a bad business. She ran away from Hamilton and he forgave it, and then she went off again. Some boyfriend of hers was driving her down to the south of France and they hit another car doing sixty, they say, and smashed themselves up. The chap's still alive but the Hamilton girl was killed outright.'

Vanessa felt a little faint. She raised her glass to her lips, trying to control her nerves. She was horribly shocked, and her mind teemed with unanswered questions. What had happened to bring about such a state of affairs between Roddy and his wife that she should have left him again within such a short time? Perhaps her South American boyfriend had found a way out of his marriage and sent for her . . . And now she was dead. All that youth and beauty — swallowed up in the grave — never to return.

Suddenly she felt that she could not sit here talking to John Brande another moment. Her mind, her heart, were too full of the thought of Roddy.

On the plea of bad *migraine*, she put an abrupt end to the dinner party, and John took her back to her hotel.

When she went to bed that night, it was to lie in the darkness without hope of sleep . . . tense . . . restless, wondering what to do . . . whether or not to try to get in touch with Roddy before she left England.

It must have been just before midnight that the telephone-bell rang, shattering the silence of her quiet room. She switched on the table-lamp beside her bed and picked up the receiver. Her whole body glowed with sudden excitement as she heard the voice of the man who had been occupying all her thoughts.

'At last I've got you, Vanessa,' he said.

'Hello! Have you been trying to get me, Roddy?'

'Yes. I only came back from France late this afternoon. I had a feeling you might be in Town and rang your hotel. They said you were out. This is the fifth time I've called you. Didn't they tell you?'

'I didn't ask for any messages. When I got in I came straight up to my room.'

'Do you know about Eve?'

'Yes. But I only heard tonight from my old friend John Brande — Colonel Brande — I think you met him once in Greece.'

'Yes. How did he know?'

'An old friend of yours told him.'

'I would have told you myself, but I had to go straight over to France, and I've been there ever since. There's been

266

so much to see to.'

'Of course. What a dreadful, *dreadful* thing, Roddy.'

'Yes, it was dreadful. She was young to die in such a violent fashion. She would go. I tried to make a show of it, Vanessa, but she wouldn't play. Her South American thought he had found some method of getting free and marrying her. So she decided to leave me finally, and join him in Cannes.'

'Roddy, I'm dreadfully sorry . . . '

He cut in quickly: 'You don't have to be sorry for me any more. I think of it impersonally. My grief for Eve has been quite curiously impersonal. It was so at her funeral. She never loved me and she cheated me right through the years. I'll tell you something. I had to go through her things. Do you remember the black fan?'

'Only too well,' said Vanessa.

'She told me that she herself had bought that. But I found a letter some chap wrote her from Madrid. Another boyfriend. *He* gave the fan to her.

Brought it home from Spain. She was no good, Vanessa. Right from the start I built my house on shifting sands.'

'Oh, Roddy, I know how you must feel, but you can start again now. In a little while you'll feel so much better about everything.'

'I feel better already . . . just through talking to you.'

Her pulses leaped.

'I'm flying back to Kenya the day after tomorrow.'

'So soon?' His voice sounded disappointed.

'I've got to get back to my job.'

A moment's pause. Then Roddy Hamilton said: 'You told me on the boat that you weren't crazy about working in Kenya.'

'I'm not, but one has to live and London offers me nothing.'

'But what about London and *me* . . . can't we offer you anything together?'

Another leap of her pulses and a wild, bright look in Vanessa's eyes. She shut them as though to savour this moment; holding the receiver tightly with slim nervous fingers.

'What exactly does that mean?'

'That if you feel the same as I do, you will chuck that job — say in a few months' time — and come back to London and me. I'm going to start my new job in a week or two's time. And I'm going to buy a cottage in the country. Do you like the country, Vanessa?'

'I love it, Roddy.'

'Then will you come back and share my cottage and my life?'

She caught her breath. Her eyes were like blue stars. 'Oh, Roddy!' she said in a choked voice.

'We still have tomorrow left to us,' he said. 'Come out with me tomorrow, Vanessa. Then I'll see you off to Kenya the next day.'

'I can think of nothing I'd like to do more, my dear.'

'Have you got a white dress?' he asked suddenly, abruptly.

'No, but I could buy one if you like

white evening dresses,' she said reck-
lessly.

'I think you'd look rather marvellous
in white. By the way, the black fan is
broken, Vanessa. I threw the pieces
away this morning. I'm going to buy
you a white one. I shall bring it to you
with some white flowers.'

Her voice when she spoke to him,
trembled on a laugh. 'Dear Roddy!
That sounds very bridal.'

'Then I hope it's prophetic — coming events casting their shadows before,
and so on. Good night, Vanessa . . . *my
darling*.'

'Good night,' she said, and put down
the receiver and covered her face with
her hands. The tears were running
down her cheeks. But her heart was
unbelievably glad.

Honeymoon Hotel

1

She thought she had never in her life seen anything more wonderful than the hotel which Rob had chosen for their honeymoon.

'Honeymoon Hotel', he called it, and held her hand very tightly as the dilapidated old car, which was the village taxi, climbed the steep hill, came finally to the top of the cliff and gave them their first view of the place where they were to spend Rob's seven days' leave.

Very tightly Ann's fingers clung to Robert's in response. It was her right hand that he held, the one with the glove on. She could not bear to put the glove on the left hand because she liked to look at her wedding ring. That brand-new little shining circle of gold. Inside it, Rob had had his initials and the words 'For ever' inscribed. She would never see the inscription again because she meant that that ring should never come off, but she knew that the inscription was there. They were such wonderful words to remember — for ever — especially when two people were as much in love as Rob and herself.

Ann had been in a state of emotional ecstasy ever since she had woken up yesterday — her wedding day. There was a confusion of delightful memories in her excited young mind, starting with the church wedding which had taken place in Chelsea, where she had lived most of her life, going on to the wonderful wedding breakfast that Mummy and Daddy had given them, and ending with the long all-night journey from Paddington to Helston in the south of Cornwall. Then the bus ride to the village of Roselyne which was the terminus. And finally the mile and a half in the taxi to the Roselyne Cove Hotel, which stood at the very end of the promontory.

It was like travelling to world's end and to Paradise. Ann opened her large blue eyes wide and gazed and gazed at the hotel as though it were an enchanted castle which might suddenly disappear from her sight.

'Oh,' she breathed. 'Rob, how marvellous! Whatever made you think of a place like this?'

Rob gave that little self-conscious laugh which was nearly always the result of any praise or flattery from Ann, and squeezed her hand all the harder.

'Oh, a chap in my squadron told me about it. He came here for his honeymoon. As a matter of fact, his people were Cornish and he was always talking about this coast. Then I saw some snaps and I thought it looked just what we wanted — right away from everyone.'

She nodded, and the sheer force of her appreciation brought a lovely colour to a rather pale young face which was insignificant save for the beauty of the eyes, and fair wavy hair, half-concealed at the moment under the blue straw hat.

Ann considered herself quite the luckiest and happiest girl in the world as she stepped out of the taxi and looked at Rob's choice of a hotel, bathed in amber light. It was breakfast time and some early bathers were already straggling in twos and threes up the path, back from an early morning dip.

Eight hundred feet below lay the sea. Ann could see the little harbour, the fishermen's boats bobbing up and down on the water and the white-washed cottages clustered around. Out in the water stood the Gull Rock. White-winged birds wheeled and circled endlessly round it, breaking the silence of the morning with their shrill and plaintive cries.

Rob paid the driver and grinned affectionately at his little bride.

'Like it?' he said. 'Sea's a jolly blue, isn't it? Like your eyes.'

'Like yours, too,' she returned, and they smiled at each other, and at the sea. Then they both looked at the hotel again. And Ann said:

'It looks an awfully expensive place. I'm sure we oughtn't to have come.'

'Silly,' he said. 'Chap doesn't have a honeymoon more than once in his life, and I've saved up for mine. No cheap boarding-house for Mrs Robert Gillan.'

Ann sighed with pure rapture. How wonderful to be Mrs Robert Gillan. She looked with utter appreciation at her husband. He wore a good grey flannel suit. He was fit and tanned after the six months he had spent with his squadron in Somerset. Rob was clever — he loved the Air Force life, and she was quite convinced that he would go a long way.

She couldn't think why he had chosen her for his wife. She felt very ordinary and insignificant. She had held an unimportant job as typist in a small auctioneer's in Chelsea. She had known Rob for years. His mother and hers had been friends and they were Londoners. They had been engaged for the last two years. She was passionately in love with him and it was the sort of love that made one feel humble. She was sure that Rob could have found someone much more glamorous and exciting than herself, but he didn't seem to want anybody else.

One of the things she liked about him best was his generosity. It was typical of Rob to have chosen a first-class hotel and a long and expensive railway journey like this. What did it matter? As he said, one didn't get married more than once in one's life. At least not unless one of them died and the other got married again, and such a thought was not possible on a morning like this one, thought Ann.

An elderly porter came out and took the two suitcases which the taxi-man had lifted out of the car.

'Good morning, sir. Good morning, madam,' he said. And that gave Ann a thrill. She had never in her life before been called 'madam'. It sounded strange and important.

'I've booked rooms,' said Rob grandly. 'Flight Sergeant and Mrs Gillan.'

'If you'll follow me, sir,' said the porter, 'Miss Taylor will see to you. The manageress is having her breakfast.'

Ann and Rob walked into the hotel. Miss Taylor, a clerk who looked pleasant and welcoming, sat them both down at a desk in the hall, gave them pen and ink and asked them to register and fill in the visitors' forms. So for the second time since yesterday Ann had the excitement of signing her new name, *Ann Dorothy Gillan*. And all the time she kept looking around her, interested in everything she saw. She caught sight of a big lounge with green carpet and little glass-topped tables and basket chairs with green cushions. And of a dining-room with little tables alongside tall windows overlooking the sea. There were flowers everywhere, and a general air of grandeur hitherto unknown to Ann. She had lived all her life in a small semi-detached villa. The only holidays she had ever spent were with the family in a cheap boarding-house in Brighton, or with Daddy's sister in 'digs', in Grange-over-Sands.

Miss Taylor said: 'We've reserved a double room and bath on the first floor for you if you'll please come this way.'

Ann and Rob walked up the stairs. The porter followed with the suitcases, and Miss Taylor led the way. A suntanned girl wearing shorts and a gay shirt, and with a cigarette between her red-tipped fingers, was coming downstairs, and stood aside to let the little party pass. Ann knew at once that she was *someone*. She had smart coloured sandals, red varnished toe-nails, and looked, thought Ann, like a film star. She was thrilled when Miss Taylor murmured to them: 'That's Lady Portlake. Doesn't she look *young*? But she's got two beautiful children. She and Lord Portlake have spent two holidays with us.'

Ann looked at Rob and whispered to him: 'Fancy, a title! We *are* in grand company.'

He answered:

'You're better than any titled woman

and better looking than that one, too.'

'This is your suite, sir,' said Miss Taylor, and flung open a door.

And then Ann did gasp, for never, never had she seen such a bedroom. It was a corner room and seemed to be all windows, looking out upon the match-less blue of the sea and the sky. The silky curtains were of rose and white design, and there were twin beds with rose and white brocade covers, cunning little lights on each head-board, and between the beds a table and a telephone. The handsome suite was of stripped and silvered wood. What a dressing-table! thought Ann, her femi-nine instincts all roused at the sight of the deep low mirror with its two wings and plate glass top. And what a carpet . . . so thick one's feet sank into it. A chaise-longue piled with cushions lay alongside one of the windows. And there was a desk with a blotter, and a box of headed note-paper. And flowers . . . two great vases of pink sea daisies, foxgloves and strange lavender-coloured flowers which Ann had never seen before.

Miss Taylor threw open another door which led from this exquisite room into a bathroom. Speechlessly, Ann went with Rob and looked at it. Their own private one . . . could anything be more thrilling? So modern and luxurious. Green tiles and green porcelain bath and green curtains with a pattern of blackbirds. And there were big green towels to match hanging over the hot water pipes. Ann thought of the bath at home, small, chipped, full of rust-coloured stains: frayed oilcloth on the floor, and patched towels that always seemed damp and uninviting, and a water system that was never really hot or adequate for a big family. When she compared it with *this*, she felt like one in a splendid dream from which she must soon awaken.

But it was no dream and now Miss Taylor, with a sidelong look at the young man, said: 'Is everything all right? Will this suit you?'

Rob said: 'Quite all right, thank you.'

And Ann said: 'It's *beautiful*.'

And Miss Taylor said: 'Breakfast is on now if you care to come down — any time up to ten.'

Then the door closed upon Miss Taylor. Ann was alone with her husband. Really alone for the first time since their wedding.

Slowly Rob came towards her and opened his arms. She went into them with a blissful sigh. Tenderly he took off the bridal hat and stroked the fair hair.

'Darling,' he said, 'my little wife. Gosh! I can hardly believe it.'

'Oh, Rob!' she exclaimed. 'It's just too heavenly. How *did* you manage to get such a room. With our own bath and all this lovely furniture. It will be something to remember all our lives.'

He gave his embarrassed laugh. 'Glad you like it. Old Tom wasn't wrong when he said the place was a peach.'

'It must cost a fortune here,' said Ann, not because she was mercenary, except in the sense that she had been brought up to be thrifty by sheer necessity, and thought it her duty to go on being so, and not to let Rob spend too much money on her.

'Oh, that's all right,' he said, 'I didn't ask for anything special, I daresay all the rooms are like this.'

'But all the husbands in the world are not like you. There couldn't be another like you,' she said ecstatically, and buried her face against his shoulder. 'Oh, Rob, it's hard to believe that there is so much trouble in the world. Isn't it all peaceful and beautiful?'

'You're beautiful,' he said huskily. 'I'm crazy about you, Ann.'

They kissed, holding each other in close and passionate embrace.

2

At the same time that Ann and Rob were admiring their room and each other, a sleek limousine drove up to the Roselyne Cove Hotel. Out of it stepped a tall slender young woman, her dark head tied up in a yellow chiffon scarf, a yellow linen suit, faultlessly cut, showing her slim figure to advantage. There was a diamond brooch pinned to the lapel of the short linen coat. She was beautifully and perfectly made up. But she looked bored and discontented. The young man with her, wearing grey flannels, looked equally bored, and was equally good-looking with his dark smooth head and deep brown eyes. His brown face wore a slight look of strain. He took off his hat and flung it into the car.

'Let's get up to our room so that I can change,' he said.

She looked with distaste at the hotel. 'You would choose a hole like this. There won't be a thing to do here.'

He looked down at the harbour and at a strip of yellow beach.

'There's good bathing and you can lie in the sun. What more do you want?'

She gave a hard little laugh. 'Oh, don't mind me. I'm just fretting after a casino and the sort of holiday we used to spend in Le Touquet, my dear Tony.'

'I wouldn't mind Le Touquet myself, but what the hell's the use of talking about it? We've used up our travel allowance and we have to wait till next year before we can go abroad again.'

'Why choose this dreary coast?'

'It isn't dreary. It's grand. Only you've got a dreary outlook at the moment, Felicity.'

Felicity Corbett took a blue enamel case from her bag, drew a cigarette from it and lit it.

'Oh, well,' she said, 'I wouldn't wonder if you are not responsible for that.'

Anthony Corbett gave a quick look at his wife and then busied himself lifting two cases out of the boot of the car. He might have known that he would be foolish to expect Felicity to enjoy a holiday in an out-of-the-way place like Roselyne Cove. Three years ago she might have liked it. But, then, three years ago Felicity had been different . . . softer . . . more contented . . . and in love with him. And he had adored her. Both of them had had money and position, but they had married for love. Why had everything changed? Why was it that there was perpetual friction between them these days, and they never seemed to get anywhere near each other? She had just accused him of being responsible for her present outlook. Up to a point perhaps she was right. He had spoiled her from the start. He had given in to every whim, and Felicity, with her insatiable love of excitement, was a woman of unending whims. Well, he had let her have her way. He had given Felicity everything she asked for. A house on the river, a *pied-à-terre* in Town, trips abroad when currency permitted. And for a time he had enjoyed that kind of life with her. But somehow, in the endless pursuit of pleasure, they had lost each other . . . grown right apart . . . and they had not found the way back.

As they walked into the hotel he said: 'Pray don't stay down here just to please me. If you are bored, go back to Town, or go away with some of your friends.'

She made no answer but yawned.

'Where are our rooms?' she asked the clerk who had just taken Mr and Mrs Gillan upstairs.

'What name please, madam?'

'Corbett,' put in Anthony.

Miss Taylor looked in her book and then nodded.

'No. 36,' she said. 'I'll take you up.'

Five minutes later Felicity Corbett stood looking in disgust at a room which seemed to her quite monstrous. It was small. It had no sea view. It had ugly curtains, a shabby carpet and that type of glazed wood furniture which made her wince. She looked with distaste at the old-fashioned double bed.

'My dear Tony,' she exclaimed, 'I must say you have made an attractive choice.'

Anthony scowled. 'It's a hell of a room, but I didn't choose it. I ordered a sea view and a private bath.'

Miss Taylor looked worried. 'There's a bathroom just across the way, sir.'

Anthony Corbett, tired and disinterested, began: 'Oh, well, if this is all you've got — '

'Don't be ridiculous,' broke in Felicity, looking very lovely with that carmine flush on her high cheekbones. 'Can you imagine us sharing a room like this? You must be crazy.'

'Can't you find us something else?' asked Tony Corbett.

Miss Taylor looked still more worried.

'There was only one front room with

a private bath vacant today, and a lady and gentleman have just gone into it.'

'But it's absurd,' protested Felicity. 'I should like to speak to the manageress.'

The Corbetts stood alone in the ugly back bedroom, while Miss Taylor went to fetch the manageress. Tony lit a cigarette and gave his wife a bitter look.

'You couldn't have put up with this even for a week with me, could you? I *am* disappointed. I hoped the spirit of romance would sweep over you and that you might hurl yourself into my arms, my darling.'

The colour deepened in her cheeks, and she cast him a look of disdain.

A moment later the manageress came hurrying up the stairs, confused and apologetic. 'I am *so sorry*. A dreadful error . . . my assistant is new and has got the bookings mixed. She has put Mr and Mrs Gillan into your suite, and she did not notice the name. I'll see that the error is corrected at once. If you will just wait downstairs, I'll inform Mrs Gillan.'

'Rather a shame to turn them out,' began Tony.

'Thank you,' interrupted Felicity coldly. 'We will have breakfast, and then perhaps you will have our other room ready. What number did you say it was?'

'It's Suite 21, Mrs Corbett. *So* foolish of Miss Taylor to have mixed the bookings.'

Felicity said: 'You go on and order breakfast, Tony, I am just going to wash.'

On her way down to the dining-room, Felicity paused on the first landing. She saw the No. 21 on a door. Vague curiosity as to what this suite would be like, made her walk up to the door and gently try the handle. It would have to be better than that awful back bedroom upstairs, or she was not staying at the Roselyne Cove Hotel, she thought. The handle answered to her touch. She pushed open the door and peered in. Ah! That was better. Quite attractive. The sooner these people got out the better.

Then a girl emerged from the

bathroom. A slim, fair-haired girl in a blue-and-white print dress.

Felicity hastily apologized. 'I beg your pardon — I was only just looking — '

'Oh, come in,' said Ann Gillan with a radiant smile. 'It's such a *gorgeous* room, isn't it? Would you like to see it?'

Felicity opened the door a little wider, stared at the other girl and then gave a short laugh. 'I don't want to disturb you but — '

'Oh, it's quite all right,' broke in Ann. 'My — my husband has gone down to breakfast, and I am just going, too. Don't you think it is the most *marvellous* room you have ever seen in your life?'

Felicity blinked. She was a little taken aback both by the other girl's enthusiasm and manner. But there was something so unaffected about it, that she could not be too critical. She murmured: 'There has been some mistake about the bookings, I think. When did you book this one?'

'Oh, Rob did, three weeks ago. Rob is

my husband. We were only married yesterday . . . ' Ann's throat and face were beautifully pink. 'We are going to spend our honeymoon here. I've never been to a place like this before in my life, and it's simply thrilling. Have you ever *seen* a bathroom like ours? . . . I *must* show you the bathroom — '

Felicity, much to her own astonishment, found herself following the little bride to the bathroom door. Ann became even more confidential.

'It's a rare treat having a room and a bath like this when you've lived with a big family in a pokey house all your life. Mummy and Daddy are wonderful and I owe a lot to them, but it is a bit trying at times to be so cooped up. This room makes you feel grand, doesn't it, and the water is so hot . . . I know I shall take three or four baths a day. Wouldn't you?' She giggled a little.

Felicity said slowly: 'I'm sure I would.'

'Oh!' sighed Ann blissfully. 'It's just like Rob to have found a place like this.

When we go home I shall be able to remember it for the rest of my life.'

Felicity made no reply. The things that this other girl was saying were making her strangely confused . . . and strangely thoughtful. Passionately she envied Ann. It must be so wonderful to come to what she, Felicity, thought a very ordinary hotel and find it so entrancing. She envied Ann her complete joy in her surroundings and her obvious pride in her newly married husband. Deep down in Felicity Corbett's heart she felt a bitter pang — and a memory — a memory of those first few weeks with Tony . . . of days before they had grown apart . . . moments when she had wanted to be alone with him and had not known what it was to be bored.

Ann eyed the tall, dark girl in her friendly fashion. 'Have you got a nice room, too?'

Felicity did not reply for a moment. She was thinking!

'Oh, lord, if I tell her that *this* is my

room and that she has got to spend her honeymoon in that lousy little back bedroom upstairs, it will break her heart. It isn't that she would mind sharing a cubby-hole with her Rob, but this is her special week, and this room with its view and its own bath . . . this is a new world for her. She has never had anything like it before. I'm damned if I am going to take it away from her . . . No, I won't, even if Tony and I have to get out and find another hotel.'

She heard Ann's soft voice. 'Are you on your honeymoon, too?'

Felicity flushed crimson and replied: 'No. I've been married for three years.'

'Oh well,' said Ann brightly, 'I expect you feel as though it's a second or a third honeymoon. I know I will if I come back here in three years' time.'

Felicity turned away speechlessly. To be so ingenuous . . . so confident of enduring love . . . so *happy* . . . This little bride didn't know how lucky she was.

'See you some other time,' murmured Felicity and fled.

She went down to the office and spoke to the manageress.

'I've changed my mind about my room. Please don't ask the Gillans to leave. Let them keep Suite 21.'

'Oh, but I couldn't,' exclaimed the manageress. 'I don't suppose Mr Gillan will wish to pay so much. It's ten shillings a day each more than No. 36.'

'To please me, will you say nothing about that, and I'll give you a cheque for the difference. I know they are not well off. They are just a little couple on their honeymoon, but I want them to have that suite.'

The manageress stared, but she did not argue. She knew all about Felicity Corbett. Everyone did. As Felicity Desborough, débutante, she had been a famous beauty, and one who was used to seeing her photograph in all the society papers, and getting her own way.

The manageress murmured: 'Well, it's a little unorthodox, but for you, Mrs Corbett — anything you like. But, of course, I can't expect you to take Room 36. If you could possibly wait until tomorrow when Lord and Lady Portlake are leaving, you can have their rooms — communicating, two singles and a bath.'

'That will be all right,' said Felicity briefly. 'Just fix that, and please — not a word to the Gillans about paying for that suite.'

Mr and Mrs Corbett breakfasted in silence. So silent was Felicity that Tony felt some surprise at his wife. She usually had something to say . . . even if it was disagreeable.

'Aren't you well?' he asked.

She was looking across the room at the Gillans. Now and then Ann looked back at her with a shy smile of recognition, but for the most part she was concentrating on the young man who sat opposite her. In fact, their gaze rarely left each other, and Felicity thought: 'I'm missing something. And it's my own fault. I know it is.'

Breakfast over, she told Tony briefly

that they were going to have Room 36 just for tonight and the Portlakes' rooms in the morning.

'Oh,' he said, astonished, 'then you aren't turning these other people out?'

'No.'

In the back bedroom with the double bed, Tony watched his wife unpack a few things and became conscious of a queer change in her.

'What the dickens is the matter with you, Felicity? What made you decide not to turn those other people out?'

Felicity, flinging a dressing-gown on to the bed, answered, 'Because they are on their honeymoon, and they haven't any money and they've saved up for this. And to that girl, Suite 21 is heaven. I'm not going to be responsible for taking heaven away from her, or from anyone else. It isn't a thing you find very often.'

Tony stared and a slow colour crept up under his tan. 'Good gracious me! I didn't think you felt like that.'

Perhaps because she was tired, or

perhaps because Ann, and everything that Ann had said, had found the vulnerable spot in her armour, Felicity Corbett burst into tears. She flung herself down on the big bed and cried as though her heart would break.

Tony, aghast, put his arms round her and held her close . . . closer than he had done for many long bitter days.

'Felicity . . . my sweet . . . Felicity, darling, don't cry. I can't bear to see you cry.'

The tears ran down her face and ruined her make-up, but she didn't care. She put her arms round his neck and sobbed: 'We couldn't have turned them out, Tony. They are so happy and that girl has never had anything like Suite 21 before in her life. Oh, Tony, I wish I were her. *I wish I were her!*'

'Darling,' he said, 'I don't want you to be anyone but yourself. And you know I'm still crazy about you only you don't seem to have had any use for me lately.'

'I've been rotten to you, Tony, but I'd

like to start again.'

He tightened his hold on her and whispered many things in her ear which she had not heard for a long time, and which were curiously comforting. He said: 'It isn't too late, darling. Let's find each other again in this horrible little room, shall we?'

'It's a lovely room,' she sobbed, 'and I'm just as happy as that girl downstairs. She asked if I were on my honeymoon, and oh, Tony, I want to be!'

'You shall be, my sweet. I'll make it the most perfect holiday we've ever spent together.'

There came a knock on the door. Tony raised Felicity, kissed her wet cheek, got up and opened the door.

The manageress was standing outside. 'Oh, pardon me, Mr Corbett, I find that we have another much better room free downstairs, if you would like it, instead of waiting for Lord Portlake's suite.'

Tony smiled and shook his head.

'Thanks awfully. We're really quite satisfied with this one now ... aren't we, darling?' He turned to Felicity.

With a handkerchief held to her lips and her eyes curiously bright, Felicity Corbett said: '*Quite* satisfied, thank you.'

The Loveliest Lady

1

When the Crisis came, Jackie decided that the whole thing was due (*a*) to not remembering her mother's favourite quotation, and (*b*) to Mistaken Kindness.

Mrs Burnett's favourite quotation . . . she so often said those words before she died, poor darling . . . used to be:

Oh what a tangled web we weave
When first we practise to deceive.

How true this was, Jackie had often discovered as a child. Not that she had ever wanted to practise deliberate deception, but there are moments of prevarication and dissembling in every child's life . . . but, thought Jackie, it never works. One is nearly always found out. And now, of course, when she was twenty, the advice still held good. It did *not* do to deceive anybody.

Jackie and her sister sat together in Jackie's bedroom in the house of her aunt, Miss Peters, with whom Jackie lived during the week while she worked. At weekends, she went down to her father's little cottage in Sussex. Colonel Burnett was now retired and, as he could not afford to keep two grown-up daughters, Rosalie, who was a year older than Jackie, ran the cottage and more often than not sat about looking lovely. But it had always been accepted in the family that Rosalie should just look lovely. She did it so well. And Jackie, who had neither face nor figure, must use her brains, keep up her end that way.

This evening Jackie had come home from the office to find a very agitated Rosalie waiting for her at their aunt's house, waving a letter and a telegram in a hand.

'Now we've gone and done it!' she wailed upon seeing Jackie. 'We ought never to have started that correspondence. The wretched man has wired *and written* to say that he's due for leave this week, and is going straight down to the cottage to see me. From this last letter, it's quite obvious that he thinks I'm just as crazy about him as he's about me, and I shouldn't be surprised if he arrives with ring and licence, and expects me to marry him at once.'

Jackie stared at her sister and said nothing for a long while. She was very tired. It was a warm, airless day in late spring ... the sort of spring that is heavenly in the country, but not so good when one has to break one's back sitting at a typewriter in a stuffy office.

She flopped weakly into a chair and faced the Crisis, not knowing whether she felt sorrier for Rosalie or herself.

It had all begun just before Christmas. Rosalie had met a young army officer who had told her of a fellow-officer whose parents had recently died and who had no other family to write to him. On the spur of the moment she had offered to write to the young man who was just leaving for Cyprus. She had enclosed one of her most glamorous photographs.

She at once received a reply from a young man named Garth Hammond (the name Garth appealed to Jackie. It summed up a man with charming qualities . . . courtesy, manliness, and a touch of the artist thrown in). He was obviously a young man of literary taste because he wrote well and profusely. In the frankest manner he praised Rosalie's photograph.

Imagine my surprise and delight, he had said in his first letter, *when I looked at that face which must surely be the face of the loveliest lady in the world. You have the most beautiful eyes, Rosalie Burnett, and behind the beauty must surely lie a kind and sweet disposition. Your photograph will make me forget the beastliness out here and remember only that there is true beauty in the world, waiting, I hope, for a fellow like myself who loves books and flowers and all things beautiful . . .*

Jackie remembered reading that note over her sister's shoulder and being extremely touched by it. One didn't expect to get an answer like that. And Jackie understood that, for she, too, loved books and flowers, and was far happier walking through the woods at home with a dog at her heels than typewriting in an advertising agency.

But Rosalie had been merely amused. Praise of her photograph flattered her. Rosalie adored being flattered. She lapped up compliments from every man she met, just as a kitten laps cream. She immediately labelled Garth Hammond 'a bit of an ass', flung the letter to Jackie and said:

'*You* answer it for me.'

At first Jackie had hesitated, but Rosalie persuaded her.

'It can't do any harm. You know how you like all this poetic nonsense, you can spout it by the yard. Carry on the correspondence for me, and let's have a good giggle when the next letter comes.'

That was so like Rosalie. She loved 'a good giggle'. Even Jackie who was loyal to her and loved her, had to admit that Rosalie's mentality was that of a shallow child at times. But with her figure, her exquisite skin, and pale gold hair, and those big melting eyes, one could forgive Rosalie everything. One did!

To be jealous was not in Jackie's nature. On the other hand she felt it was a bit hard that she should not have had more of Rosalie's attraction. Hers was such a slight, nondescript figure, such ordinary brown hair, which had no intention of curling naturally like Rosalie's and she had what people called 'a nice little face'. What was the good of that? Men swarmed round Rosalie like flies round a honeypot, and it was always, 'Be a sport, Jackie, and get Rosalie to come out,' or, 'You're a good kid, Jackie, do ask Rosalie to ring me up.'

Well, she had made the mistake of upholding Rosalie too far this time, for in commencing that correspondence with Garth Hammond, she had set alight a fire in him — and in herself — that would not easily be put out. Jackie had grown to hunger for every letter that came from Cyprus, and thirst for the moment when she could sit down and write to Garth — to someone who so completely understood her. He *did* understand, and he said that she was the first woman in the world to be in complete spiritual touch with him.

★   ★   ★

I walk with you through your beloved woods, he had written in one letter last week, *and so well have you described them, that I can shut my eyes while I rattle along on a lorry in the white dust, and see the carpet of bluebells, hear those gay-throated blackbirds calling, and smell that unforgettable odour of dry leaves and*

bracken, and wild thyme. Oh, Rosa-
lie, I don't think it's fair that you
should have been given so much
. . . a lovely face as well as such a
lovely mind. You don't know how
I'm longing to meet you.

That had been the jarring note.
Those last few lines. There was always
something that spoiled every one of his
letters for Jackie. Always the name
'Rosalie', and the allusion to her
physical perfections.

But Jackie had gone on writing,
learning more about him, his ideals and
his ambitions. And they all seemed to
be in sympathy with hers. They both
wanted the Right Person and a cottage
in the country — winter or summer,
they both loved the country.

But each letter that came made
Rosalie giggle all the harder. She
couldn't be bothered with 'that stuff',
she said. Her ambitions were to find a
husband with money and have parties
and exploit that lovely face and figure

of hers to the utmost. Garth was obviously not the man for her, but she liked the idea of the scent which he had said he had bought for her. And things became quite serious when in one letter he mentioned that, as he had nobody to leave anything to, he was going to make a Will in favour of her just in case he was killed in Cyprus.

Well, if there was one thing Rosalie liked it was money, and since Garth Hammond wished to leave her what little he possessed, let him get on with it, she told Jackie.

It was after this letter that Jackie began to realize the gravity of what they were doing. Second-Lieutenant Garth Hammond was obviously not a young man to be trifled with. He had a sense of humour, every letter proved that, but one couldn't stretch a man's humour as far as this. He was in love with the beautiful Rosalie of his imagination, and when he came home he expected to find that same Rosalie who had written to him, grown near and dear to him.

This evening, reading the last letter which had just come from Garth, seeing that telegram which announced joyously that he would be home on leave tomorrow, Jackie felt aghast.

You do not know what you have done for me, Rosalie. It just makes my leave seem worth while. It will be heaven after being out here. You've grown to mean everything. Even before I see your lovely face in actual fact, I want to tell you that I love you. There could be no other girl in the world for me. I want you to marry me, Rosalie . . .

Utterly dismayed, Jackie read this letter. Her heart was thudding and her eyes misted over and there was a horrid feeling of anguish in her heart. For if only *she* had been Rosalie. If only it was true that Garth Hammond felt like this about her, what heaven it would have been for her! She had never been in love in her life before, but she was in love with this young officer whom she had never met and whom she knew so well; who, after their almost daily correspondence had ceased to be a stranger. For, as he so often said, it was as though they walked side by side through the woods and talked and laughed together.

But it had all been a mistake and a grave one at that. For he would come home to find that the Rosalie of his dreams bore no resemblance whatsoever to the real Rosalie.

In despair, Jackie looked at her sister.

'What are you going to do?' she asked. 'Will you go on pretending that it was you who wrote the letters?'

Rosalie glanced at her reflection in the mirror, pushed a fair silken curl into place, then examined one slender ankle reflectively.

'Of course not. I couldn't live up to all that twaddle. I'll just tell him that the whole thing was a joke. He might like to take me to a dinner and show.

We could have some fun together on his leave. After all he ought to be pleased to step out with what he calls 'the loveliest lady' . . . '

'Oh, stop!' broke in Jackie, and suddenly put her face in her hands and began to cry, quite helplessly and hopelessly. She couldn't bear to hear Garth made a mock of. She couldn't bear the thought of his coming disillusionment. And most of all she could not bear the thought that he would be furiously angry — and rightly so — with *her* — for practising such a deception upon him.

Rosalie was perturbed at the sight of her sister's collapse. Jackie was always a cheerful, placid person. If there were ever 'scenes' at home it was she, Rosalie, who made them. Jackie must be very upset to cry.

'My dear sweetie-pie, surely it doesn't *matter* to you, does it?' she asked.

Jackie raised a passionate young face, disfigured by tears.

'It does, it matters *terribly*. Garth

Hammond is in love with you, and I'm in love with *him*. Yes, I admit it, and if he saw me . . . '

She sprang to her feet and looked at herself in the mirror.

'Imagine if he saw *that*. Me! When he's had your photograph nailed by his bedside and written odes to your golden hair and your perfect mouth . . . *Oh*, I could die of shame, and of misery! I shall never face him. You'll have to. You'll have to tell him the truth, but I shan't be in when he calls.'

Rosalie frowned, read Garth's telegram, then yawned a little.

'It started as a joke, but it's become a bore,' she said. 'I'm sorry if you've fallen for my lonely soldier, Jackie dear. But maybe if he doesn't like my face sufficiently, he might be wooed over to yours. I'll ask him — '

'You'll do nothing of the kind,' broke in Jackie passionately. 'I'd rather die than have him handed on to me from you. I just hope I'll never meet him, never hear from him again . . . '

'I shouldn't take it so seriously,' said Rosalie with another yawn.

Jackie's tears dried up. She took the cigarette that Rosalie offered and smoked it in grim silence, but the pain in her heart ached on. Never now would she and Garth walk through her woods together. Never would she be able to show him her silver birch, the willow by the pond, the Saxon monastery half a mile from the cottage, where nothing was left but an archway of grey stones, purple aubretia tumbling out of the crevices. A flowering thorn and tangled herbs growing in what had once been the monks' garden.

Garth Hammond had wanted to see it all. He had often talked of that walk in his letters. Now it was all over and the jest was to end in tears.

Rosalie had no intention, however, of making her mascara run with a single tear. The thing didn't seem tragic to her. She felt that she could tackle Garth Hammond once he came. He'd only have to look at her to fall for her even when he knew she couldn't write a decent letter if she tried, and that the country bored her to tears, but that she preferred doing nothing in the cottage for the moment, to getting up and working like Jackie.

When Jackie spoke again, her young voice was as grim as her face.

'When do you think he'll turn up at the cottage?'

'Tomorrow, or Saturday. He says 'arriving weekend'.'

Jackie bit her lip.

'I shall go down tomorrow afternoon to see Daddy and get a few things and then come back here.'

'I suppose you *can* fall for somebody through a packet of letters,' said Rosalie, 'not that I could. I think you're being a bit silly, and I expect when we see him we'll hate the sight of him.'

'I shall never see him,' said Jackie.

And upon that she was determined. For she knew that she could never hate the sight of the writer of those letters . . . dozens and dozens of them which

Rosalie had received and laughed over, and thrown away, and which *she* had kept and read again and again, cherishing every word. Long after Rosalie had left her — she was going on to a dinner and show with one of her admirers — Jackie sat alone thinking about Garth. She shuddered to imagine his reactions when he discovered the truth. On the other hand, with a touch of cynicism, she wondered whether he would be content with Rosalie's loveliness, and dispense with that spiritual companionship of the last three months.

And now, suddenly, for the first time in her life, furious, futile jealousy shook her. She sat at her dressing-table staring at her small pale face. She said:

'You're *really* plain. Plain next to Rosalie. You couldn't be 'the loveliest lady' to any man. It was even a farce when they christened you Jacqueline. You're just Jackie, and *he* wouldn't like that name, anyhow.'

There came to her mind a paragraph

in one of his letters, most of which she knew by heart:

Last night in the mess, a fellow was playing an old gramophone record, and a man was singing 'Rosalie, my darling', and it ended up with the words 'Rosalie mine'. Loveliest of names for the loveliest of girls. God! If I thought you were mine, I'd be the happiest man on earth.

He was in love with the Rosalie of his imagination and she didn't exist. That was the irony of it.

2

Jackie, running along the platform to catch her train down to East Grinstead that Saturday afternoon, felt that Fate had conspired against her these last twenty-four hours to make her thoroughly unhappy.

There had been a row at the office. Some papers had been lost. Jackie was responsible and she had got into a row. It *was* her fault, because she had been so distrait the whole morning, and instead of typing columns of figures she had found her mind wandering, longing to write the name Garth . . . to explain to him . . . to sink pride and just say:

Don't go out of my life. Forget Rosalie and walk with me through my woods and let me hear you say all the lovely things you have written.

322

The row had made her late for lunch and now, of course, she almost missed her train. A guard saw the slim young figure in grey flannel suit tearing down the platform and swung open the nearest door of a first-class carriage:

'Hop in, miss.'

Jackie practically fell into the carriage, falling over the suitcase which fell at her feet with a thud.

A man's voice said: 'Hold up,' and a firm hand under her elbow supported her swaying figure. For a moment she had a confused glimpse of a tall young man in officer's uniform, then sank into the seat opposite him, and was horribly ashamed to find that the tears were welling into her eyes. She was tired and depressed, and had never been so miserable in her life.

The young officer seated himself opposite her and, after giving her a brief look, interested himself in his paper.

Jackie looked round the compartment, in which they were alone, and blurted out: 'I suppose it's all right since the guard put me in here, but I've only got a third-class ticket.'

The officer put down his paper and smiled. 'I'm sure it'll be all right. These trains are very full.'

Miserable though she was, Jackie, being a hundred percent woman, was bound to notice that this young man had a very engaging smile, and although not strictly handsome, had a brown attractive face, rather on the thin side, and eyes that were a striking shade of blue.

After a moment he pulled out a cigarette-case and offered it to her.

It was not Jackie's habit to make friends quickly with strangers, but if there was one thing she needed at the moment it was a cigarette, and she hadn't had time to buy a packet. Gratefully she took one.

The young man lit it for her and said: 'Marvellous day, isn't it?'

'I suppose so.'

He jerked his head in the direction of the window. 'Well, just look!'

She looked. Of course it was a perfect day. Blue sky, with little fleecy clouds. Warm sunlight. Already a glimpse of green fields and banks massed with yellow primroses.

Spring! How she loved spring in the country. Usually, Saturday was a red-letter day because it meant two days at the cottage. But this weekend had a black outlook. Just an hour or two in her beloved garden and then back to London to escape Garth Hammond.

'It's good to get out of Town, isn't it?' observed the young officer (his voice, she noted, had a pleasant boyish quality).

She sighed deeply: 'Yes.'

He added:

''Oh to be in England
Now that April's here.''

'It isn't 'here'!' said Jackie dully. 'It's 'there'.'

He was amused and interested. 'I believe you're right. I stand corrected.'

The faintest smile lifted the misery from Jackie's mouth. 'Sorry, but it's a favourite quotation of mine and I often argue about it.'

'Are you fond of poetry?'

'Not all. I like verse about Nature in particular.'

'So do I.'

And suddenly Jackie was drawn from her slough of despond and began to talk to the young man who certainly had plenty to say on his side, and with some enthusiasm.

He, too, began to enjoy his journey. At a first glance he had thought the girl in the grey flannel suit nondescript . . . a fellow wouldn't look at her twice. But now he was not so sure. When she smiled, it lit up the small pointed face, and she had a very expressive pair of soft grey eyes. There was something rather touching about those eyes . . . a wistfulness that reached one's heart.

For the first half of the journey, they discussed a variety of things. But now they were past Redhill and had come upon the glory of green woods and daisy-starred meadows where white woolly lambs drowsed by their mothers or frisked about on their absurd spindly legs, jerking absurd tails. The young officer stared dreamily at this picture of rural England and said: 'Lord knows why anyone lives in London. I see you're sensible, you get out of it when you can.'

Jackie, who had been almost enjoying her conversation, suddenly remembered everything and sank back into a welter of misery.

'But I've got to leave it all tonight and go back to the beastly city.'

He smiled at her in his friendly way. 'Oh, you just couldn't.'

'I must — I daren't stay at the cottage tonight. I'm frightened of meeting someone.'

His blue eyes twinkled. 'That sounds intriguing. Who on earth can frighten you away from Sussex-in-the-Spring?'

Her cheeks coloured. 'I — can't very well tell you.'

He leaned forward and now his eyes were grave. 'You looked so happy just now when you were talking about the spring. I hate to see anybody look miserable. Do smile again,' he said.

His unexpected gentleness, and the personal note which had crept into their discussion, completely floored Jackie. To her horror the tears, which had been threatening all morning, surged back to her eyes, brimmed, and trickled down her cheeks.

Hastily the young officer pulled out a khaki handkerchief. 'Take this,' he said, 'it's clean.'

'You must think me a fool,' she gulped, refused the handkerchief, pulled out one of her own and blew her nose forlornly.

'I think you're awfully nice,' he said.

To his astonishment, Jackie flared up into what might be called a passion.

'Oh, I'm *sick* of that word! I don't want to be *nice*. I want to be beautiful, marvellously beautiful like my sister. Oh!'

And then she was sobbing aloud and the young man was sitting beside her, patting her head and saying: 'Look here! Look here, this won't do at all. I say, you're not to cry any more. I know something's wrong. Just tell me about it. You've no idea how good I am at keeping secrets.'

Jackie raised that 'nice little face' knowing perfectly well now that it was spoiled by her tears.

'All right, I will tell you,' she said almost defiantly. 'I'm never likely to see you again, so I *can*. It's all my fault. I did an awful thing. I pretended to be someone else and this is the consequence.'

He had lit a cigarette for her and put it between her fingers gently. Incidentally he thought what charming little hands she had. They looked kind and sensitive with nails not too pointed and varnish not too red.

Then he sat back and found himself listening to the story she blurted out. As he heard it, his face changed, his whole body stiffened and a look of incredulity came into his eyes. But when she paused, he said: 'Go on: You say you can't face this fellow because you're ashamed of what you've done.'

'Yes.'

'Why are you ashamed?'

'Because I know it will hurt him. His letters were so sincere. He has fallen in love with his ideal of Rosalie. He believes in her and expects to find her ready to take him to all those places they've written about to each other. And she won't. She will want theatres and dances and supper — we're absolutely different . . .'

'But why did this . . . Rosalie . . . allow you to write her letters for her? She must be a callous young woman. Did she just want a kick out of the poems the lonely soldier wrote in reply or the perfume he bought for her?'

'Oh, Rosalie's really very sweet, but she's just thoughtless,' said Jackie loyally.

'Personally,' said the young man, 'I

330

think she's been thoroughly selfish. So you're ashamed because you think you've hurt Garth Hammond. And what about being hurt yourself? You say you've fallen in love with him?'

Jackie looked blindly at the sunshine.

'I've got to forget that. But now you see why I'm running away from the country tonight. I *couldn't* face him. And yet he's the one person in the world I most want to see.'

A pause. Such a long pause that Jackie wondered why her newfound friend made no reply to her last statement. She turned and saw him sitting with his hands locked, shoulders slightly bowed, and brows knit as though in deep thought.

'Do you think it's awfully silly?' she asked timidly.

Then he turned and gave her a queer look.

'No. Not silly, just . . . very touching, and do you know, Jackie . . . ' he used her name as though he were accustomed to it ' . . . I think you're rather a coward not to face up to Garth Hammond and tell him the truth.'

'It isn't that. I'm not *afraid* to face him . . . only afraid to see him hurt. He must be an awfully nice person from his letters . . . the sort of man nobody should hurt wantonly.'

His blue eyes searched her face.

'Do you never think of yourself, but always of others?'

She did not answer, but shook her small brown head forlornly.

He added:

'By the way, do you know your Yeats . . . he talks about loving a woman's beauty, and he also says: 'But one man loved the pilgrim soul in you and loved the sorrows of your changing face'.'

Her heart beat unevenly. 'Why do you quote that?'

'Because I think that great beauty is a wonderful asset to a woman, but it is useless without that 'pilgrim soul'; that spiritual side. And spiritual beauty can make any woman lovely, if a man is *looking* for real loveliness.'

She put her hand against her lips. 'Garth Hammond might have written such words.'

'Garth Hammond has just said them,' he said abruptly.

Jackie sat motionless and stared at him with eyes that were large and bright with astonishment. An astonishment which changed to dismay.

'*Oh!* Oh, it can't be true. You're not Garth. I haven't been telling it all to *you*.'

'Yes, my dear, I am Garth.'

Burning and red, the blood crept to the roots of her hair. 'How *awful*.'

Yet she read neither disgust nor anger in the blue eyes which looked at her. Only the same kindliness which had been there before — and something else. Something deep and tender.

'How lucky, I would say,' he observed, 'lucky that I chose to take this train to East Grinstead, and that you got into it. Just Fate, Jackie, but it would have been an unkind Fate if I'd never met you, and if I had been welcomed home for my leave by . . . Rosalie.'

Jackie could hardly think straight, her emotions were so chaotic. But *of course* this was Garth, she told herself. It couldn't be anybody else. It was Garth as she had pictured him, the voice, the smile, everything.

'Oh, why don't you tell me what you think of me,' she burst out. 'Go on! I'm not a coward. I can take it.'

'I will tell you if you like,' said Garth Hammond. 'I think you're very sweet and very honest and really quite adorable. I think that possibly the only wrong thing you've ever done in your life was to send that photograph of your sister to me instead of your own, and so put me to the infinite trouble of having to accustom myself to the fact that my future wife's name is Jackie, instead of Rosalie.'

Back went Jackie's fingers with that nervous gesture to trembling lips.

She gulped. 'You can't mean that.'

'My dear,' he said, 'haven't I just told you that beauty is only worth having when there is a soul behind it? I like that funny little face of yours and I positively adore your mind and all those things you've written to me. I know all about you. I knew a lot when I was in Cyprus, and as I told you, I have been looking for a long time for someone with a mind like yours. It's so perfectly in tune with my own.'

She made no answer, she was too stupefied. But when his warm strong fingers took hers, and she felt the touch of his lips against the back of her hand, a thrill of purest happiness shot through her whole being. The eyes she lifted to him were so starry bright that he caught his breath.

'Darling,' he said, 'and you said you were not beautiful! Jackie, you're not going back to London today. You're going to show me that silver birch . . . and the willow by the pond . . . and the woods . . . aren't you?'

'Oh, I just don't know what to say or think,' she blurted out. 'I've wanted to show them to you so much.'

'Then why not start? And we shall get to know each other all over again.'

'But when you see Rosalie . . . '

'I shall, without doubt, meet a glamorous girl in whom I haven't the slightest interest. I wrote those letters to *you*, Jackie, not to her. And it is to you that I have come back on leave.'

'Really me?'

He kissed her hand again.

'Really you . . . my loveliest lady!'

A Family Affair

1

It was generally agreed amongst the first-class passengers on board the ship which docked at Southampton a week before Christmas, that there could not be a happier couple than Captain and Mrs Richard Pursell — nor a luckier.

They seemed to have everything. Looks, money and that grand addition to the family, young David. David, aged six, had a pink chubby face in spite of having spent the last four years of his life in the Middle East, where the climate during the hot weather wasn't supposed to be too good for little boys. But it didn't seem to have hurt David. Neither was his seemingly angelic nature spoiled by all the petting that he got during the voyage from Port Said.

Few could resist those large limpid eyes — blue, like mother's — with her long curly lashes. Nor that mop of reddish golden curls which were also an inheritance from the maternal side. But the shape of his face, the squareness of his little shoulders and something in his wide cheerful smile were directly bequeathed from his father.

Up till forty-eight hours before the liner reached Southampton, both Finella and Richard Pursell had thoroughly enjoyed the voyage.

That evening, Finella kissed David, left him tucked up in his little bed in the cabin which he shared with his nurse and two other women, and changed for dinner. There was a dance on board tonight. It was awfully cold after the Middle East. Finella hadn't stopped shivering since they had left Gibraltar, and she quivered a bit at the thought of putting on a thin evening-dress. But she adored dancing and especially with Richard, even if it meant keeping on her fur coat.

She was feeling at the top of her form when she entered the cabin where Richard was already bathed and half-dressed.

'Darling!' said Finella, 'you *are* in good time. I'm late. I've been telling David Christmas stories and he wouldn't let me go. He's so excited because it's the first real English Christmas he can remember.'

'Well, it looks to me,' said Captain Pursell, struggling with a black tie, 'as though we shall all be spending it in London.'

Finella's brows went up.

'No, we won't. We're going down to The Old Forge.'

Richard Pursell cleared his throat.

'Well, I'm not sure now, darling. There's a cable over there on the bed.'

Finella picked up the cable and read it. The gaiety which had lain in her lovely eyes a few moments ago, vanished. She frowned.

Meeting boat with car Stop Expect you all Christmas.

Father.

'Of course, that's absurd,' said

Finella. 'They're expecting us at my home.'

'Well, darling, it's a bit difficult. The old man hasn't seen me for two years. We spent our last summer leave with your people while Dad was in Kenya. I think we really ought to go to him this time. Especially as he's so keen to see a bit of David.'

'He can see David as much as he likes after Christmas. Mummy and Daddy are counting on us taking David down to The Old Forge. Besides, a country Christmas is so much more fun.'

Richard Pursell grimaced at his very good-looking reflection in the mirror while he tied his tie, then carefully smoothed a lock of dark hair back with a stiff brush.

'Oh, I don't know, darling. After all, we *did* spend the summer down in Sussex, and Dad's house may be in London, but it's a grand old place and I spent many a Christmas there when I was a lad . . . I'd rather like David to hang up a sock in the dining-room under the portrait of his great-grandfather.'

Silence from Finella. She stood there, very straight and slim in her green dinner dress, looking, thought Richard, quite adorable. He was still very much in love with this young wife whom he had married seven years ago, but who was still in his eyes the enchanting bride of twenty who had taken him 'for better for worse'.

He dropped his brush, went up to her and pulled her into his arms.

'Take that cross look off your face, sweet. It upsets me.'

But for the first time since he could remember, Finella avoided his kiss and pushed him away.

'Well, I'm upset. I'd absolutely counted on Christmas down in Sussex and Mum and Daddy will be horribly disappointed.'

'But, darling, so would the old man be disappointed.'

'He can come to The Old Forge, too.'

'You know perfectly well, my sweet, that General Richard Pursell never moves from his own fireside, except to take a trip once every three years to Nairobi to see Aunt Sue.'

'Well, then it's very selfish of him,' said Finella, coldly. 'I don't see why he shouldn't break the rule and join our family party down in Sussex for a change.'

Richard moved away, hurt by Finella's rejection of his embrace.

'Well, darling, if it comes to that, aren't you being selfish? Why shouldn't you bring David to spend Christmas at my home and go down to The Old Forge on Boxing Day?'

'It's *Christmas* — I want with my people,' said Finella, stubbornly.

'I see,' said Richard.

And after that there was a ten minutes' silence. Richard lit a cigarette and smoked it. Finella carefully touched up her make-up.

This was the first serious altercation which had ever taken place between the

Pursells after seven years of complete understanding and happiness, and the argument continued while Finella finished dressing. It could, of course, they both realized, have continued all night if they allowed it. They had reached deadlock. Each of them wanted to spend Christmas with their own people. Each was justified; neither one more than the other. Neither would give in.

Matters were made a bit worse by the tactless conduct of a certain William Trevor who was on board, travelling home from Australia.

Bill Trevor was not in the Army. His job lay in 'wool business' in Melbourne. From the moment the Pursells had stepped on board at Port Said, Bill Trevor had 'spotted' Finella and claimed her as an old acquaintance. He, too, came from Rushwood, Finella's home-town in Sussex. Finella had told Richard that 'poor old Bill' had once been very much in love with her, and had never married because of it. But she hadn't looked at him. She had never looked at any man except Richard. Richard was well aware of that and had never been jealous of Finella in his life. She was a devoted wife to him and a marvellous mother to David. He had been mildly amused to watch the said Bill Trevor 'mooning' about the boat in vague pursuit of Fin.

But tonight Bill's pursuit was a little less vague. After a rather hearty dinner and quite enough whisky, he openly expressed his admiration for Mrs Pursell. She looked exquisite, he announced, in that sleek green evening dress. He pestered her for dances. And as Fin was not feeling in a good mood with Richard, she gave more dances to Bill than she intended and many more than she wanted. He was a poor dancer, anyhow, compared with her Richard.

Towards the end of the evening, Finella was extremely depressed. She felt that the whole voyage had been spoiled by the arrival of General Pursell's cable. In consequence it made her feel quite antagonistic towards the old man. She wished Richard wouldn't keep aloof from her and look so stern, so *wooden*. She wished he would come and seize her out of Bill's arms and make her dance with him, but he didn't. And finally, after dancing with a few acquaintances whom they had met on board, he disappeared.

Bill Trevor said: 'What's bitten our noble captain? Is he sore about something?'

'Oh no,' said Finella, briefly, 'we're just having an argument as to where we spend our Christmas.'

'Why, Fin, you're spending it down in Rushwood, of course,' said Bill Trevor. 'It's going to be grand fun seeing you back in the village, and me on leave at the same time. A bit of a break for me.'

Finella, dancing with him, looked at him through her long lashes. He was quite good looking, old Bill. And they used to be great friends. Played a lot of tennis, bathed, picnicked, rushed round the country in that awful old open

Bentley which used to make so much noise that it woke up the whole countryside. And then, Bill, falling in love, had spoilt it all, and simultaneously Richard had come along. He was at Aldershot at that time. She had gone down to a dance, and at once given her whole heart to that lithe, six-foot-one of attractiveness in mess-kit. There was something about Richard that a woman couldn't help loving. She would go anywhere in the world with him. Gladly put up with all the petty inconveniences of being an officer's wife; moved from pillar to post. And with the arrival of David, their happiness had been complete.

And now they were *quarrelling*.

Finella suddenly stopped dancing, bade a brief good night to Bill and went down to her cabin. It was in darkness. Richard was evidently asleep. And had not even said good night to her, she reflected bitterly.

Had he been awake, Finella had meant to fling herself into his arms; to shed a few tears, and to tell him that she would go anywhere for Christmas, even disappoint her people if he wanted her to. But now his neglect had upset her all over again. Men were hateful, un-understanding brutes. Richard ought to have been pacing up and down here, waiting for her to come, and continue their discussion; wanting a reconciliation. He ought to know how hurt she was. He ought to realize, too, how utterly she had set her heart on going down to Sussex with David this Christmas . . . And instead . . . he had gone to bed and to sleep . . . without kissing her good night!

Finella undressed, got into her narrow bed and shed those tears all by herself, until the gentle movement of the ship, the rhythmic creaking, the sound of the sea outside the porthole sent her, also, to sleep.

2

The coldness which sprang up between husband and wife that night was still existing when the P & O liner moved slowly into Southampton docks. They were on what might be called 'speaking terms'. When David was present they laughed and talked as usual. They even kissed each other good night. But there was none of that passionate warmth, that lovely intimacy which had hitherto constituted their marriage. They were strangers, refusing to see each other's points of view. When the argument about Christmas came up, Richard always had plenty of reasons why they should remain in London with his father, and Finella had many others for going down to Sussex to her people.

David didn't know about it and didn't care. His interests lay entirely in the thought of hanging up that stocking on Christmas Eve, being taken to Harrod's to see the Toy Fair, and making a snowman.

It was an intense joy to him because it was actually snowing when they got off the boat.

'One of the coldest Decembers we've had for many a year,' was General Pursell's remark, when he met his son and daughter-in-law, and the chauffeur took their luggage and put it in the Daimler which was waiting for them.

'Good to see you again, Dad,' said Richard Pursell heartily.

'Grand to see this youngster, too,' said the General, looking through his eye-glass at the youngest Pursell. 'He gets more like your mother every day.'

'Oh!' said Finella. 'I think he's much more like my side of the family, really.'

'Well, well!' said the General. 'You're all spending the week with me at Chester Terrace, I hope.'

Finella and Richard exchanged glances. Richard mumbled a non-committal answer.

He really didn't know what to do. They hadn't reached any conclusion yet. He felt wretched about the whole affair. He wanted to please Fin and call a truce between them. And yet . . . why should she be so confoundedly selfish about going down to Sussex with the boy?

Finella was no happier than her husband as the car bore them slowly towards London. The chauffeur wouldn't drive fast. The roads were slippery. England lay under the pale grey pall of winter. The snow-flakes were whirling down from a leaden sky. Ugh! it was cold. Finella drew her furs closely about her and tucked a rug around David, who howled with joy every time they passed a field white with snow.

'We'll make a snowman! We'll make a snowman!' he cried ecstatically.

'You can make lovely ones in Granny's garden,' said Fin, stealing a covert glance at her husband.

Richard's handsome face retained its wooden expression. He refused to join in the conversation. He and his father launched into a discourse on world affairs, the political crisis, and Richard's own job. He was going to the Staff College. He and Finella expected to settle in Camberley for the next year or two.

But at the back of Richard's mind he had an uncomfortable picture of his wife in her jade-green evening dress dancing in the arms of that fool, Bill Trevor. He *was* a fool. Thought of nothing but fast cars and what he called 'beating it up'. Richard didn't know how Finella could have ever made a friend of Bill. Surely she liked someone a bit more serious-minded. And Trevor lived down in Rushwood. If they went down there for Christmas he'd be hanging around, no doubt. Not that Richard mistrusted Fin, but the mere presence of Trevor *annoyed* him.

'I want to see Granny and make a snowman!' came from the youngest Pursell.

The General tweaked his moustache and smiled benignly upon his grandson.

'You'll be seeing her soon, my boy . . . ' He turned to Finella. 'Going down to your people next week, eh?'

Then Finella took the bull by the horns.

She was fond of the General. She had always got on very well with him and considered herself lucky that she had no interfering mother-in-law. But she was not going to be *made* to spend her Christmas away from The Old Forge this year . . . her first Christmas home for a long time.

'I do hope you won't be too disappointed,' she said, 'but you know we promised to spend Christmas down in Sussex.'

'Nonsense!' said the General.

And that, of course, brought an angry flush to Fin's charming face, and the colour ran up under Richard's tan. There followed a very uncomfortable half an hour of gentle but determined argument between the three of them; none of them willing to surrender.

By the time they reached London,

Finella was feeling nervy and altogether upset. As soon as she was alone with Richard in the bedroom which had been allotted to them in the big house in Chester Terrace, facing Regent's Park, she broke out stormily: 'I'm not going to be bullied. Mummy and Daddy are expecting us on Christmas Eve and I'm not going to disappoint them. I just haven't the heart. Besides, I want David to have a real English country Christmas and that's that.'

Said Richard haughtily: 'Surely the whole of Regent's Park is good enough for David to build snowmen in?'

'Well, I think it's absurd to argue this way. I've never really gone against your wishes before, but I'm going to now. I'm taking David down to The Old Forge, and that's final.'

A moment's silence. Richard looked a little white about the lips. Then he said: 'Very well. If you have made up your mind, you must go. But I shall stay here with the old man.'

'You mean you'll be separated from

David and me?'

'I don't want to, but you leave me no option. I see no reason why the poor old boy should spend a lonely Christmas, and he won't go down to The Old Forge so it's no good bringing that up again. Naturally I shan't like not being with the kid on Christmas Day, but I'll join you on Boxing Day, and now for heaven's sake, let's stop bickering. I hate it.'

Finella swallowed. Tears were stinging her eyelids. It seemed so awful for Richard to speak to her in that cold and unfriendly way. He had not given in to her altogether. Merely capitulated. And in a way his arguments were justified. She could see that. But she did not like the alternative he gave her. It was all very well being down at her old home with David, but without Richard — why, it would be horrible!

Once again she was on the verge of giving up her own wishes. Had Richard made one loverlike gesture then, she would have surrendered. But he was annoyed, and when Richard was annoyed he showed it. He walked out of the room, adding over his shoulder: 'Make my apologies to the family and explain that I just can't leave my father alone.'

'Very well,' said Finella, tossing her head, 'we'll leave it at that.'

And there it was left. And the matter was not referred to. The General, having been told that his daughter-in-law and grandson were not remaining here, was upset but made no effort to dissuade Finella from going. It was Richard's business, and he wasn't going to interfere.

When, however, the moment came for Finella to say goodbye to Richard — he put her and David and Nanny on the train at Victoria on Christmas Eve — she was filled with misgivings. She wished she wasn't going. She wished Richard would come. She wished anything but that they should be separated for Christmas.

For a moment, just before the train

went out, she hung on to her husband and raised a woebegone face. 'Darling, I hate this, really . . . '

'So do I,' he admitted, and gathered her closely to him.

One kiss . . . the first really passionate one since that dispute on the liner . . . and the guard blew his whistle.

Through a haze of tears, Finella saw Richard's figure growing smaller and smaller as the train moved out of the station. She did love him so much. He would hate it, really, alone in that great London house with the General. Ought she to have stayed? But no, he ought to have come with her.

Surreptitiously she wiped her eyes and then sat down and turned her attention to David, who was kneeling on the seat, looking out at the snow-white world.

Then David suddenly said: 'Where's Daddy?'

'He isn't coming with us, dear,' said Finella. 'He'll come later.'

The smile was wiped from David's

face. 'But I want Daddy. He's going to make me a snowman.'

'Nanny and I will make you one, darling.'

'I want Daddy to make it. He knows how.'

'So do I, dear,' said Finella patiently.

The corner of David's mouth turned down. 'I want Daddy. He said he'd make me a snowman.'

There followed a slight argument with Master David. He had some of the stubbornness inherited from his parents. And when finally he was made to understand that his father would not be with him for Christmas, he lost his interest in the snow and in his journey, and sat still, pouting, muttering that he 'wanted Daddy'.

Finella felt quite desperate by the time they reached Rushwood. Everything was going wrong. Even David was going to start being difficult now. The sight of her beloved Sussex village and the eager faces of her father and mother who were there on the platform to meet her, could not altogether raise her spirits. For she realized quite definitely that after all her dreams and hopes, this Christmas was not really going to be a success.

3

On Christmas Eve the sun came out and the snow-covered village of Rushwood glittered as though encrusted with diamonds.

Finella, looking out of the drawing-room window of The Old Forge, thought what an unreal fairy-world she gazed upon. A real 'Christmas card Christmas'. Difficult to believe that just over a fortnight ago she had been sitting in the club without a coat, drinking cocktails with Richard and watching people bathe and play tennis.

She had loved her life in the Middle East with her husband and her small son. But more than anything in the world she had looked forward to this Christmas at home — her old home. There was no lovelier house in Sussex than The Old Forge. Malcolm Garner, her father, a retired solicitor, had bought it thirty years ago when it was a dilapidated wreck of Tudor architecture, but full of magnificent beams, open fireplaces, and wonderful old yew floors. Today, restored and enlarged, it was a goodly sight standing there in an old garden which made a perfect setting for it. They were high up, and on this bright December afternoon could be seen the sweep of the Sussex downs. Finella was waiting for David to come back with Nanny and have tea. Her mother was lying down and Mr Garner had put chains on his car and driven into Horsham to buy something very special for the Christmas-tree which was being prepared for David.

Finella turned from the window and looked at the drawing-room. Holly behind the pictures. Mistletoe in the doorway. David's tree waiting there in a corner shrouded in dark mystery, hung with tinsel, paper chains, and mysterious packages, the tiny scarlet candles ready to be illuminated tomorrow.

Wistfully Finella looked at the silver

star at the top of the tree. Stars always made her think of Richard.

'Your eyes are like stars,' he used to say to her when they were first engaged. Not a very original remark, but she had loved it, and he had given her a diamond brooch in the shape of a star for her wedding present.

She had missed Richard dreadfully these last twenty-four hours. She really wasn't going to enjoy this Christmas without him and she was sure he would be missing her and David. He ought to be here instead of doing his duty to that old man up there in the big empty London house.

The sound of an approaching car drew her to the window again. This must be Mr Garner returning from Horsham. But it wasn't. It was a stream-lined sports car and out of it jumped a tall man in grey flannels and tweed coat with a scarf round his neck.

Finella grimaced to herself. Bill Trevor again. Bill had been haunting the house ever since she arrived in it.

She was bored by him. He seemed to think that just because she was here without Richard she was open to a flirtation. But he was wrong. It was stupid of him to try and recapture those old days when they had been boy and girl together.

Bill came into the house, hearty and pleased with himself, rubbing his hands.

'Merry Christmas, Fin.'

She almost snapped at him: 'It isn't, 'til tomorrow.'

'Well, who cares? The sun's shining. How about having a crack round in the car?'

'No, thanks, Bill. I'm just going to have tea with David.'

'Heard from the husband?'

'Yes, thanks.'

Finella lied. She hadn't heard from Richard since she had left London. But she wasn't going to tell Bill. She walked back to the window and looked down the drive. How lovely the trees were with the powdery snow lying on the branches like delicate white lace. David was late. Nanny had taken him on to Rushwood Hill to use his toboggan. A homemade affair, knocked up by the gardener's boy. She hoped he hadn't damaged himself. She wasn't the sort of mother to worry unnecessarily about her child. She didn't believe in it. But Nanny was supposed to be back before four. The sun was going down. The short winter afternoon would soon be drawing to a close.

She had been a little anxious about David last night. Despite the combined efforts of his mother and grandparents to give him a wonderful time, he just had not been himself. It wasn't a question of health. He was quiet and preoccupied. He kept asking when 'Daddy was coming'. She knew he adored Richard. But she hadn't expected the child to make quite such a fuss about being separated from him. Not that she didn't understand. Her sympathies were all with David. She felt that Christmas would not be

Christmas without Richard.

She tried to make conversation for Bill, but he could not hold her attention. In half an hour's time, when the afternoon had darkened and it looked chill and grey outside with none of that fairy-like splendour which the sun had created, she grew really worried about David.

'I'm going to look for him,' she announced.

Bill volunteered to accompany her. In fur coat and gum-boots, Finella trudged through the snow to Rushwood Hill.

Eventually she found Nanny, but not David. Nanny had a man from the village with her, and she was crying. She looked raw with cold. She immediately blurted out a long story about David having tobogganed by himself to the bottom of the hill and vanished.

Finella, her heart sinking, shot a question at the girl.

'But how on earth *can* he have vanished?'

Nanny said that he 'just did'. She

found his sledge there, but not the small boy. Of course, there were woods around and he might have run into them. She had shouted and hunted for him, then Tom Smithers from the grocer's had come and helped her look. But there was no trace whatsoever of David.

Bill Trevor saw Finella's face grow as white as the snow. He took her arm and pressed it.

'Steady on, old girl. He can't have gone far. Let's go back to The Old Forge and pick up my car. We'll soon find the little chap. He's playing some sort of game.'

Finella bit a quivering lip.

'I know exactly what's happened. He's run away. He's run away to find his Daddy.'

Nanny sniffed.

'He hasn't done anything but ask for his father the whole afternoon. I shouldn't be surprised if you're not right, Madam.'

Without a word, Finella turned and

began to run through the snow towards home.

'Come along, Bill. We're going to get your car and find him.'

4

About half an hour before David Malcolm Pursell vanished from his nurse's sight, his father stepped out of the train at Horsham station and deposited a suitcase in the luggage office.

'I'll come back for it with the car later,' he said. 'I'm going to walk to Rushwood now.'

It was a four-mile tramp across the fields to his wife's old home. He knew every inch of it. He loved the country and he wanted a walk. He also wanted to surprise Finella and the boy.

It was soon after lunch that he had made up his mind that he just could not stay away from Fin and David for Christmas. It *couldn't be done*. Dash it all, he had felt confoundedly mean and guilty from the moment he had seen them off at Victoria yesterday. He had

369

been haunted by the wistfulness in Fin's eyes. Perhaps it had been unreasonable of him to expect her to stay in Town when she had promised her people to take David down to them.

He tried to persuade the General to go to Rushwood with him, but the old man would not move.

'You go down, my boy. I understand. I won't be offended or anything like that. Your place is with your wife and boy. Go down and come up with them later in the week.'

And soon after that, Captain Pursell had packed and caught the next train to Horsham.

Now he felt happier than he had done since that wretched argument with Finella on the boat. Everything had been rotten since then. He was longing to get back to her, take her in his arms, recapture some of the perfect happiness which they seemed to have lost. No, not lost, he told himself, just temporarily mislaid. But tonight, Christmas Eve, they would find it again.

He breathed deeply of the invigorating air as he walked through the crisp snow. It was cold when the sun went down, but he still enjoyed the walk. He took the short cut which eventually led him to the gate through which he let himself into the orchard of The Old Forge. It was too dark now to see anything much but the welcome beacon of lights from The Old Forge windows. He was aching to see Fin . . . to hear David's shouts of: 'Hullo, Daddy!' This would be the dickens of a surprise for them. They had no idea he was coming.

Hands in his overcoat pockets, Richard Pursell walked round to the front of the house. As he did so, the big studded oak door opened, letting a shaft of light out into the drive. It lit up an open sports car. At the same time, the driver of the car switched on his headlamps, and now Richard could see who was at the wheel. Bill Trevor. And out of the house came Finella in a fur coat, with a scarf tied over her curls.

Richard, who had been about to leap

forward, stood still, unseen in the darkness. All his eager anticipation of meeting his wife died down and in its place came a wave of resentment and jealousy.

So she was going out alone with that fellow on Christmas Eve. Consoling herself in her husband's absence and leaving the boy, *on Christmas Eve*. Altogether unlike Finella!

He heard his mother-in-law's voice: 'Take care of yourself and the best of luck. Don't worry too much.'

Then from Mr Garner: 'Sure you wouldn't like me to tell Richard?'

From Finella: 'No. Not yet, it isn't necessary. Don't spoil his Christmas Eve . . . '

With this, Finella jumped into the car and slammed the door. Bill Trevor started up the engine and the car disappeared down the drive.

Richard stood motionless. He was blank-eyed and baffled. What on earth did they mean, all of them? *Why* was Finella going off with Bill Trevor at this hour? *Why* did they wish her luck? And *why* in heaven's name did she say that he, Richard, wasn't to be told? Told *what*?

He made a movement as though to step forward. Then heard his mother-in-law speak again, just as she shut the front door.

'Oh, Malcolm, what a thing to have happened on Christmas Eve! What *will* Richard say!'

The front door closed. There was darkness and silence in the snow-covered drive.

5

For a moment Richard stood still and irresolute.

There were two things that he could do. Walk straight into the house and demand an explanation, then commandeer his father-in-law's car and try to follow Finella and Bill. Or do nothing about it at all. Wait for Finella, herself, to offer an explanation of her extraordinary behaviour.

Richard Pursell was a proud man. It was pride which made him choose the latter course.

Nothing would induce him to face his 'in-laws' at this moment. It would be too humiliating. Besides, if what he feared was true, it was altogether too staggering and too unbelievable. He could not face up to it. Not just now. He must have time to think things quietly out.

Hands deep in his pockets, he turned and began to walk through the dusk back to the station whence he had come.

It was a long, lonely, bitter walk for Richard. No sound except the crunching of the caked snow under his shoes. He walked like a man in a trance. He felt, indeed, as though he were in some nightmare from which he must soon awake. He loved Finella, his wife. With all his soul he loved her and the boy. It had never entered his head to suspect her of infidelity. When they had parted such a short time ago, she had seemed so unhappy about leaving him. Those limpid eyes of hers had been full of tears. He had come down to Rushwood tonight believing that he could soon have her in his arms and that they would, as always, spend their Christmas together. The two of them — and the boy.

How could Fin have done this thing to him? *And* to David? Poor little chap! There he was, on Christmas Eve, alone with his grandparents, while his mother drove off *with her boyfriend.*

At those last two hateful words which leapt into Richard's mind, he stood still. He went hot from head to foot. His heart began to thump strangely and a queer kind of dizziness attacked him. He drew a hand across his eyes and for a moment breathed very deeply. He felt almost as though he were choking. He was not a neurotic or hysterical kind of man. He was particularly cool and practical. But the mere notion that Bill Trevor might seriously be his wife's boyfriend — that she might be in love with Bill — hit him like a blow which momentarily drove sanity from him.

He wasn't going to stand for this. And it wasn't true. It *couldn't be.* There was some awful mistake. He was misjudging his wife. And as for Bill Trevor . . .

Richard Pursell turned and began to run back towards his father-in-law's house. He had already covered a couple of miles across the fields to the station, but he retraced them like one frenzied.

He must get back and talk to the Garners, find Finella, talk to her, see David; *anything*, rather than spend this Christmas Eve alone with his awful doubts and fears.

He reached the stile which was the boundary of the pasture-land belonging to Rushwood Farm. Stepping over it, his foot slipped and he fell heavily and got up with a muttered oath. He had twisted his ankle a bit. He began to limp rather slowly now down the main road towards The Old Forge. The night was very dark. There were neither stars nor moon. And against his face whirled softly big snow-flakes. They brushed his eyelids like invisible fingers.

He was a sorely perplexed and unhappy man as he covered the rest of that mile-age. His mind literally teemed with jealous thoughts about the wife he adored.

Then suddenly, reaching the bottom of the drive which led up to The Old Forge, he heard a sound which made him stop and listen intently. The faint pitiful sound of sobbing. A muffled, unhappy kind of sobbing, and it came from a small figure which Captain Pursell could only faintly discern in the dark. But indistinct though it was, Richard recognized that figure instantly. *It was David, his son.* David, in the short reefer coat, muffler and beret which his mother had bought for him the moment they reached London.

'David!' exclaimed Richard.

The small figure flung itself precipitously into the arms of the tall man who had loomed so suddenly out of the darkness. There was a wild shout of: 'Daddy! *Daddy!*'

Richard Pursell lifted his small son up into his arms and hugged him closely.

'Why, David, darling, what the deuce are you doing out here? You're frozen, absolutely frozen, old chap.'

David Pursell put a cold, tear-wet face against the warm one of his father. He continued to sob. In between the sobs he said many things to which Richard listened, but could divulge little beyond the fact that David had been looking for him. And he had been looking for the last three or four hours. That was why he was so cold. The small boy had had no tea, and had been wandering desolately through the woods, and round the countryside hoping that he would find his father.

'Now you can make me a snowman,' were David's last words, uttered on a note of deep gratitude because his prayers had been answered. He clung with two raw little hands about his father's neck.

Carrying that small figure, Richard began to walk quickly down the drive. He felt thankful beyond words that he had come back and discovered the child. From what he could gather, nobody in The Old Forge knew where David was. Richard felt furiously angry with them all, and especially with Finella. Obviously her behaviour had driven the boy out. Possibly David had seen or heard something about his mother's intentions of going off with Bill Trevor. No doubt that was why David had run away.

Richard comforted his son and put a complete end to the crying.

'You've nothing to worry about now, old chap. Here I am, and here I stay. *Of course* I won't leave you. And by jove, we'll be hanging up that stocking in a minute. Tomorrow's Christmas Day. You haven't forgotten that, have you?'

David hadn't forgotten and he said so, smiles replacing the tears.

A few moments later, Captain Pursell marched into the warm lighted hall of The Old Forge and deposited David on his feet.

Mr and Mrs Garner rushed out of the drawing-room, took one look at the small boy and broke into exclamations of relief.

'It's David! David's come back!'

'Richard! What are *you* doing here? How did *you* find him?'

Rather coldly, Richard addressed his 'in-laws'.

'I came down unexpectedly to surprise Finella. I found the boy outside, half-frozen and afraid to come in.'

'Oh, the poor lamb!' said Mrs Garner, and gathered him in her arms.

'What did you mean by running away like that, you little imp?' demanded his grandfather.

Mrs Garner, kneeling beside David, peeling off his coat and scarf, looked up at Richard.

'You didn't by any chance run into Finella and Bill?'

The muscles of Richard's face tightened.

'I did not.'

'The poor darling! She went off half-demented with worry. She and Bill are scouring the roads for David. How *can* we get in touch with them?'

'They'll be back if they don't find the boy,' said Mr Garner. 'I don't think it's any use us going after them. We'll only miss each other.'

'How wonderful for Finella to find both of you here, when she gets back, my dear,' added Mrs Garner, patting her son-in-law's shoulder.

No answer from Richard. The frozen

look in his eyes had thawed. Incredulity and astonishment gave place to the light of understanding. For now he could see the whole thing. What a confounded fool he had been! And what a complete nit-wit even to suspect Finella. She hadn't run away with Bill, or anything near it. She had merely gone out with him to try to find the boy. *That* was what she had meant when she had said that he, Richard, 'wasn't to be told, because it might spoil his Christmas'. She had been trying to save him from worry because David had run away.

The reaction was a bit too much for Richard Pursell. For a moment he saw his 'in-laws' and his small son through a kind of haze. He clutched Mr Garner's arm.

'Could you find me a spot of whisky, please, sir?'

'Why, Richard!' exclaimed Mrs Garner. 'You look *green*.'

Richard Pursell gave a shaky laugh.

'I don't know about being green, but I feel . . . all kinds of a fool.'

But he wasn't going to tell Mrs Garner why.

He allowed his father-in-law to lead him into the dining-room and pour him out a stiff drink. And while he drank it he closed his eyes and thanked God for this ending to the torment which had so stupidly racked him half an hour ago.

That whisky was hardly down his throat before Finella and Bill Trevor returned home. Finella in tears because she had not traced her son. Bill Trevor looking sheepish and distressed for her sake.

And it wasn't long after that, alone in their room, Richard held his wife in his arms, and was kissing away her tears with an ardour which even Finella could not quite account for.

She, herself, was almost hysterical with joy at finding David safe and sound and none the worse for his escapade. And she was overjoyed to see her husband here at The Old Forge. It was the last thing she had anticipated. But she did not quite understand why Richard kept asking to be forgiven.

'Darling, forgiven for *what?*' she questioned him.

'Not coming down here with you in the first place,' was Captain Pursell's answer. (Of course he knew that wasn't quite the case. Silently he was asking Finella's pardon for having doubted her . . . for having thought all those things about Bill Trevor. But he was always a man of tact and he saw no reason whatsoever for distressing her by confessing to his jealous suspicions.)

He kissed every inch of Finella's face before he let her go.

'I think I'm more in love with you than ever tonight, Fin,' he said huskily.

Finella patted his cheek, drew a deep breath, and pushed back her tumbled curls.

'Darlingest! I'm just exhausted with emotion. It's been the most amazing Christmas Eve.'

'It's going to be the best we've ever spent,' he said, putting an arm around her and walking with her towards the door. 'Now let's go along to the nursery and hang up that stocking with young David.'

'He ought to be spanked for running away,' said Finella, with a little laugh. 'But I'm afraid I can't blame him, poor sweet. I felt like running away myself to find you. Oh, Richard, darling, *listen*!'

They stood still a moment with their arms around each other. From the distance across the snow, came the sound of bells ringing from Rushwood Church. And downstairs, outside the front door, some village boys had started up a carol, in quavering, uncertain young voices.

'While shepherds watched their
   flock by night,
All seated on the ground . . . '

Finella and Richard smiled into each other's eyes.

'Let's go down and give them a shilling,' she said.

'Let's go down and give them two,' said Richard.

It Might Have Been

1

Julia Leardon looked across the breakfast-table at her husband — she could see nothing of him but the pair of brown, strong-looking hands that held the morning paper — and wondered gloomily whether all marriages must come to this. Disillusionment and boredom for the wife, and apathetic indifference on the part of the husband.

There sat Freddie — just as he sat nine mornings out of ten — so oblivious of her presence that he would barely notice whether she got up and walked out of the room. Not because he had ceased to love her. Oh no! In his way he still cared for her deeply she was sure, and, when questioned, he assured her of the fact. But after ten years, a fellow couldn't keep up the honeymoon spirit, he said. A woman shouldn't expect it. One couldn't live at fever heat. All these books and stories that said so were sentimental twaddle. Yes, he said that, and a lot of other things like it. And remained just what he was — a good and faithful husband. A hard-working soldier, devoted to the Army and crazy about games. Organizer of most of the big hockey matches, and in every respect an ideal member of any club in any military station.

Julia, thinking things over in her mind this golden morning, was doubtful as to whether she was the right wife for Freddie. Yet once she had thought herself so absolutely right for him, and Freddie for her. They had been madly in love when they had married. She had stayed in love until his gradual decline from the impetuous lover of the honeymoon, to the prosaic husband of today. The romantic streak in Julia was strong and deep. It took a lot of eradicating and for years she had hoped that Captain Freddie Leardon might some day become again the adoring subaltern whom she had married at Aldershot.

But now her hopes were at an end. These last six months in the Middle East had spelt nothing but disappointment for her. When the regiment had been drafted out to this station, she had anticipated a glorious awakening of the romantic feeling between them. This was the land of glamour and mystery. Amidst the beauty of burning deserts, shining Nile, in the heat, the splendour, the excitement of the oldest civilization in the world mingling with the new, surely life could begin again for them? Freddie would revive the passionate tenderness he had once lavished upon her. He would come back to her joyously, ready with flowers, with kisses, with appreciation. He would make her feel twenty-four again, instead of thirty-seven; almost *middle-aged*. Yes, that was how he made her feel these days. It was a mental rather than a physical thing, because she had lost none of her looks. Her figure was a little plumper perhaps, but her mirror told her that she was still beautiful. This climate suited her. The sun had warmed her skin to a gorgeous tan and bleached her hair to a shining halo of silvery curls. She didn't *look* her age. She knew that, and Freddie's brother-officers paid her a lot of attention. Besides being attractive to look at, she played good tennis, good bridge, and she could be amusing when she tried. Freddie had *nothing* to grumble at. But then he didn't grumble. He just neglected her. He *slept* in her presence. He seemed enthusiastic only about the Army or his wretched games. And his passionate moments were so rare and brief, they had become a question of habit more than anything else.

'I *want to be loved again!*' was the silent cry of her heart, and it was a cry that Freddie did not hear.

Julia finished her grapefruit and stood up. The grinning Sudanese in his white robe, and with a red tarboosh on his woolly head, moved forward with a dish of bacon and eggs. She motioned him to serve the captain and walked to the window and gazed out with discontented eyes. Another glorious day. The sky was so blue that it made one's eyes ache. From the window of their 'quarters' she could see a scarlet flamboyant — a garden full of English flowers. The dusty green of trees — cool and green on this hot sun-baked morning. A car went down the road followed by a native leading a donkey and cart.

'I'm like that car,' thought Julia, bitterly . . . 'I want some speed and excitement and thrills of my youth . . . and Freddie's like the donkey, unseeing, uncaring, *stupid*. Oh, I would hate him if I didn't love him so much.'

Resentment bubbled up in her furiously. She swung round and said: 'Do stop reading that paper.'

Captain Leardon dropped the local *Mail*. He was smiling a little. The rag was always full of misprints and some of them made him laugh. Now what was the matter with Julia? Was she in one of her moods? She had been pretty moody lately. Sulky as hell about nothing. Perhaps the heat tried her a bit. He didn't know. He didn't understand her very well. But then how could any man understand women — damned unreasonable, illogical creatures.

'Stop grinning!' said Julia.

Freddie attacked his bacon and eggs. 'Don't be silly,' he said in a mild tone. 'Why shouldn't I grin?'

Julia clasped her hands together. 'You don't care what *I'm* feeling, do you?'

He looked up at her. How good-looking he still was, she thought. No one would think he was nearing forty and just about to get his majority. He was still the boy she had married — lithe, clean-limbed, with rough brown hair that stuck up a little on his head, and charming, friendly eyes. She had always loved that grin of his, too. It seemed tragic that it should irritate her this morning.

'My dear Ju!' he said. 'I don't happen

to know what you *are* feeling.'

'Fed up with you!'

'Oh, lord,' said Freddie, and returned to his breakfast.

Tears suddenly sprang to Julia's eyes. They were brown, soft-looking eyes. Years ago Freddie used to tell her how marvellously they contrasted with her blonde head. Today she wondered whether he would notice if they had turned blue in the night.

'I honestly don't think you love me any more!' she said in a muffled voice.

'Oh, lord,' said Freddie again, 'how can you be so silly?'

'I'm not silly. But you've *changed*.'

Freddie laid down his knife and fork. His thoughts were not really upon love. He was thinking that the servant boy hadn't put the proper shine on his buttons this morning. He felt irritable. He wanted to take off his belt and throw it at the boy. And here was Julia behaving in the most untoward manner, accusing him of being no longer in love with her. Of course he was. But dash it all, a chap had other things to think about than telling his wife all day how much he loved her. Important things connected with his job; and, by the by, he mustn't forget to talk to the adjutant about Corporal Cooper. The poor fellow had been taken to hospital with an appendix. They'd have to find another goalkeeper for next Saturday's hockey match.

Through the jumble of his masculine thoughts came Julia's tearful voice: 'Say what you like . . . I *know* you've changed! You never want to take me out by myself now. I believe you'd have forgotten it was my birthday the other day if that cable from Mother hadn't reminded you . . . and you know I wanted to go into town and dance and see the Continental cabaret this week. Estelle and Leroy are dancing . . . Oh, you're *beastly*! . . . '

The voice broke off. Julia had turned and rushed out of the room.

Captain Leardon drew a deep breath, raised his brows and returned to his

Mail. Certainly, old Julia was in another of her moods. Of course, *she* was a bit temperamental — always had been. But he thought he understood her. She'd be quite all right when he got back this evening.

Later, the captain took his hat and cane and prepared to drive out to the conference. First of all he opened the door of Julia's bedroom and put in his head. She was lying on her bed crying.

Compunction seized Freddie. He hated to see Julia cry. He walked up to her, ruffled her fair head and said: 'Well, cheer-ho, darling. Buck up! And don't be such a little idiot. See you later.'

No movement from Julia. But after the front door closed, she stood up, dried her eyes and considered bitterly that men as a sex were unfeeling, unsympathetic brutes. So Freddie could see her cry and just say: 'Cheer-ho' and tell her not to be 'a little idiot'. Yet the Freddie of ten years ago would have been on his knees at the bed saying some of those marvellous things he used to say. Such things as: 'I can't *bear* to see tears from you, my darling. Oh, how I love you! Cry in my arms if you must, but not out of them.'

Well, she was out of them now all right. And back he would come from the camp this afternoon ready to make an odd joke or two, ignore this morning's scene and accompany her to the colonel's for bridge tonight. He couldn't begin to see how she missed the lover he used to be. Well, perhaps she *was* an idiot. Perhaps she was making herself ridiculous at her age, behaving like a schoolgirl. Or, perhaps she'd teach Freddie a lesson and find somebody who *did* want to bring some glamour into her life.

Julia walked to her dressing-table and made up her face. She even went so far as to contemplate putting a telephone call through to a certain young subaltern who had shown her marked attention when they were all dancing at the French Club at a party last weekend. *He* would appreciate her, if Freddie didn't.

Then she remembered that a friend of hers, a major's wife, Evelyn Forcett, was coming to tea. A special date. That was a bore. She would really rather have gone to the Tennis Club and had tea and a game of tennis with her young admirer.

Julia thought of her husband. And she knew even as she stood there, that she didn't want anybody to admire her except Freddie. Her tears broke out afresh.

2

Captain Leardon walked out of the hot sunlight into the cool hall of his quarters in which a fan was whirring; wiped his face and neck with a large khaki cotton handkerchief, and cursed the climate. It was much too hot for work today and yet it *would be* the one day when the colonel had wanted him to do a spot of extra work, and had kept him in the office until half past three. At this time of day he expected to have a siesta. He had meant to take Julia over to the beach for a swim, too. He had felt a bit worried about Julia when he had time to think of her, this morning. He had begun to wonder whether she was just moody or really unhappy. Had he *really* been neglecting her? Ought he to wake himself up a bit and do something about it?

He handed his uniform cap and cane

to his suffragi and said: 'Anyone at home?'

'Lady at home and Mrs Forcett.'

Freddie grimaced. He liked old Forcett but Evelyn was a bit of a bore. One of these organizing women — always getting things up. Tried to rope Julia into every committee meeting or charity fête in the area.

Freddie changed from his uniform into grey flannels and walked into the sitting-room, prepared to be as civil as was necessary to the wife of a senior officer. He paused to tuck a silk handkerchief into his coat pocket. As he did so, he heard Julia's voice. A voice so fraught with misery that it gave him a shock. And what she was saying gave him a far greater shock. It froze him to the marrow.

'You see, my dear, I don't want to tell him. It wouldn't be fair to him to learn the truth about me. Can you imagine what he'd feel if I told him that I had only three months to live?'

Freddie stood motionless, spellbound, the colour draining away from his cheeks under their healthy tan.

Julia with only three months to live! Good God, what was she talking about? Rooted to the spot he stood there. He heard Evelyn Forcett's rather high, metallic voice replying:

'But, darling, I think he ought to know. Anyhow, is the doctor sure?'

'Quite sure. I saw the best man in London. He said nothing could save me. Even if I went to Switzerland it wouldn't help. In fact I might as well stay in my own home. I prefer it. One lung's gone and the other's seriously affected.'

'But did you only have one opinion?'

'No; two — and they agreed.'

'You *must* tell your husband, darling.'

'No, no,' came from Julia on a note of hysteria. 'I'll never do that. It would make me much worse if he knew. I want him to be happy. I love him so much, I couldn't bear to see him suffer over me. I suppose in time, as I get worse, he is bound to discover, but for the present it makes me happier for him to be left in ignorance. My poor old darling . . . I can't bear to think of leaving him alone.'

Her voice broke. There was silence. All Freddie heard now was the sound of sobbing; then Eveyln said: 'You're the bravest person I've ever met. Too wonderful for words. I'm sure I'd have told my husband in your position.'

Freddie, with the look in his eyes of a man who had received a mortal blow, turned away from the drawing-room, staggered back to his bedroom, sat down on the edge of the bed and put his face in his hands. For a moment he did not move. His feelings were indescribable. He only knew that what Evelyn Forcett had just said was true. Julia *was* the bravest person in the world. It couldn't be true that she was only going to live another three months. His Julia who so loved life. Julia with her charming smile, that fair silky head without a grey hair in it . . . Julia with her exquisite colouring. He remembered how mad he had been about her delicate colour when he first fell in love with her. Now he could see that it was all too delicate. It was the flush of a consumptive. And that cough she had had last winter. The MO had not been concerned. But she *had* been to see the doctor in London during their last leave. She had received sentence of death at that visit and had carried it off with a smile. She had gone on smiling. Anything, rather than let him know. Anything to spare him agony.

Now he began to understand her moods; her appeals to him to be the lover of old times. And he, brute that he was, had just chaffed her and remained stolid and unimaginative.

Freddie beat a hand against his forehead. Never, *never* would he forgive himself for causing Julia pain. For reducing her to tears this morning, for instance. He was all for rushing into the drawing-room and telling her that he *knew*. But something held him back — the memory of her own words:

'*It makes me happier for him to be*

left in ignorance.'

All right, he wouldn't let her know that he knew. He'd do something for *her* this time. Until she was actually so bad that she couldn't conceal it, he wouldn't tell her what he had over-heard. But, by heaven, he'd make her happy. He'd cram happiness into every remaining hour for her. Every hour she had left. He'd make her see other doctors, too. He'd just say, casually, that he didn't think she was very fit, and ought to be overhauled.

For an hour, Freddie sat there, brooding, marvelling at the courage of a woman, and vividly conscious of the passionate love that he still bore his wife. The mere idea of losing her was insupportable.

He could not bear to face those two women in the drawing-room. He slipped out of the flat and went for a walk. With unseeing eyes he walked into the Tennis Club, acknowledging people whom he knew, in automatic fashion. There were crowds drinking tea on the lawn. The tennis courts were full. The sun glittered down on the green palms, the golden bignonia that tumbled in a lovely cascade over the verandah of the club, the roses that were in full bloom this glorious March weather.

Freddie used to love the garrison — as he loved his military life altogether. But today, everything seemed dark and sinister. For Julia was under sentence of death. Julia, his heart's darling.

He was in a calmer mood when later that evening he returned to his flat. He had schooled himself to master his emotions, up to a point. Definitely he was going to respect Julia's wish that he should not know the truth about her. He realized that it would be better for them both, otherwise they would break down continually — unable to enjoy anything, with the shared knowledge of that disaster hanging over their heads.

He found Julia in the sitting-room drinking a gin-and-tonic. His heart contracted as he looked at her. She seemed especially beautiful tonight, in that mist-grey chiffon dinner-dress, with coral bracelets on her arms. Her cheeks were flushed. (Now he realized how much too hectic that colouring was!) The next moment, unable to help himself, he strode across the room and seized her in his arms.

'Oh, my darling, how sweet you look,' he said, huskily.

Julia had had a bitter remark on her lips ready to reproach him for not coming back in time for tea, and to show him that she was not going to stand his indifference any longer. She was so amazed by his reception of her that she could not speak. But she felt his arms about her and his lips against her eyelids, closing them with kisses in a way that he had not done for years. Speechless, she stood in his embrace. He went on kissing her, murmuring all kinds of ridiculous things.

'Do you remember when I gave you those bracelets, Julia? . . . when we were stationed in Singapore I bought them for you . . . Just after we were married.

It doesn't seem so very long ago; my darling . . . my sweet . . . '

Julia blinked her long eyelashes. She gasped: 'Freddie, what on *earth* has come over you?'

He wished he could tell her, but dared not. He said: 'Nothing, Julia, nothing, darling, except that I've realized I've been behaving abominably. I love you and I want you to know that. Just as much as I always did. I've been neglecting you. I know it. But I'm going to get leave at Easter and take you to Italy. You haven't been looking well. We'll rake up the cash somehow. We'll fly to Rome and then go to Venice. You've always wanted to go there, haven't you, darling?'

Julia went limp in his arms. She was too speechless, too staggered to reply very coherently. She only knew that a miracle had happened; that Freddie had come to his senses and realized that he was missing something by being the complete husband, and had become her lover again. The young, ardent Freddie who used to make life so rapturous for her. She was too sensible to question him, and too much afraid of spoiling the precious moments by making recriminations. With a blissful sigh she surrendered herself to the longest kiss she and Freddie had exchanged for a very long time.

That night, Freddie Leardon tried to forget the horrible truth that his wife was a dying woman. Every time she coughed he winced. It hurt him so that he had to clench his teeth. Yet he was happy. It was strangely good to be Julia's lover again. To see her eyes shining at him, and to realize how much she cared after all their years together.

He forced himself to be gay. Somehow or other he managed to sit through the Bridge party at the colonel's. But he scarcely took his eyes off his wife, and Julia's heart sang within her. It was just too wonderful to be back on these terms with Freddie. Time and time again he thought: 'If only I could have these ten years over again. If only I hadn't wasted them! And now there are only three months left. I'll never, *never* forgive myself.'

He refused to take her home after the Bridge party. They would go on to the French Club, he said, and have a few drinks and a sandwich, and dance. Julia loved to dance.

'You're sure it won't hurt you?' he asked. And then was terrified that she might guess what he had discovered. But she did not appear to do so. She just laughed and said:

'Why should it? It's been such a lovely evening. Like old times, darling. Let's go on making it lovely.'

They danced at the club until late. And even then Freddie would not let the evening end. He took her on to the one and only night-club — at the George Hotel — and they danced there, cheek to cheek, like lovers, while a Greek girl crooned French songs in a dreamy soulful voice. Once he whispered to Julia: 'Happy?'

Julia, with eyes like stars, answered: 'Terribly. Oh, Freddie, I'm still so much in love with you! and I do believe you've fallen in love with me again.'

'I have,' he said brokenly, and wished in that hour that he could die for her.

Driving her back to the Garrison he pulled up to light a cigarette. The moon was wonderful. A native voice sang sadly, poignantly through the night, drifting from Arab Town.

Julia, snuggled against Freddie's shoulder, said: 'I've always thought this the most wonderful place in the world, even in the hot weather. Tonight I *know* it is.'

He put an arm round her. 'Baby-heart!'

She closed her eyes. He hadn't called her *that* since the days in Singapore. She felt drowsy and utterly content. She said: 'Do you know, until now I thought you were getting tired of me, Freddie.'

His clasp of her tightened. 'Never, never, my darling.'

'You seemed so disinterested in me.'

'You must forget it, Julia. I've been a

fool. Tied to my job. Thoughtless. I want to make up for it.'

'You've made up for it tonight,' she whispered.

'Tell me what you'd like to do.'

'When?'

'Oh — just in the near future. I'm due for leave.'

'I'd like to go to Italy — to Venice, as you suggested. But we can't leave here until after the show.'

'What show?'

'You know — the theatricals Evelyn Forcett and I are getting up for the regiment.'

'You did say something about it,' Freddie said vaguely, 'but you're not to go working too hard with that organizing female. What's she making you do?'

'Just a play. You know she came this afternoon and we had a rehearsal. I've got the part of a girl who is dying of consumption. It's quite tragic' — Julia laughed — 'I keep the truth most nobly from my husband. Three months to live and all that.'

It was the second shock that Freddie Leardon had received that day. He took it straight on the jaw. Silently he sat there, his arm still round his wife's shoulder. He did not know whether to howl with laughter or break down and weep against her breast. He felt a complete fool. Worse than a fool. Yet this relief was so terrific that it exhilarated him to the highest pitch. Julia wasn't dying. *Julia hadn't got consumption at all*. All his agony, his fear had been for nothing. He had merely overheard a rehearsal between herself and Evelyn Forcett — the rehearsal of a play.

But it had brought him face to face with one vivid fact . . . the fact that he was still in love with his wife, and had forgotten how to show it. Forgotten the joys of loving.

And it might have been true that Julia was dying. *It might have been*.

He began to shake. Julia stirred in his arms, and said: 'What is it, darling?'

He laughed aloud then, intoxicated

with the sudden joy of the knowledge that Julia was going to live . . . that in all probability they had another twenty years of happiness left to them. He said: 'Nothing, darling. I just feel on top of the world, that's all!'

'So do I,' she said, drowsily. 'Give me a kiss and then drive on, darling. Let's get home.'

We do hope that you have enjoyed reading this large print book.

Did you know that all of our titles are available for purchase?

We publish a wide range of high quality large print books including:
Romances, Mysteries, Classics
General Fiction
Non Fiction and Westerns

Special interest titles available in large print are:
The Little Oxford Dictionary
Music Book, Song Book
Hymn Book, Service Book

Also available from us courtesy of Oxford University Press:
Young Readers' Dictionary
(large print edition)
Young Readers' Thesaurus
(large print edition)

For further information or a free brochure, please contact us at:
Ulverscroft Large Print Books Ltd.,
The Green, Bradgate Road, Anstey,
Leicester, LE7 7FU, England.
Tel: (00 44) 0116 236 4325
Fax: (00 44) 0116 234 0205

Other titles in the
Linford Romance Library:

MISTRESS OF MELLIN COVE

Rena George

When Dewi Luscombe is rescued from a shipwreck by the young Master of Mellin Hall, Kit St Neot, she finds she has lost her memory and doesn't know who she is. Touched by the girl's vulnerability and confusion, Kit decides to help her. But Dewi is haunted by the thought that someone close to her died in the shipwreck, and she sets off with Kit to ride across Cornwall to discover her true identity. Will Dewi ever regain her memory? And will Kit return her growing feelings for him?